THE ADVENTURES OF
ELLIE & BOO

THE ADVENTURES OF
ELLIE & BOO

MILLIE KERR

ILLUSTRATED BY EVE O'BRIEN

The Book Guild Ltd

First published in Great Britain in 2020 by
The Book Guild Ltd
9 Priory Business Park
Wistow Road, Kibworth
Leicestershire, LE8 0RX
Freephone: 0800 999 2982
www.bookguild.co.uk
Email: info@bookguild.co.uk
Twitter: @bookguild

Typeset in 11pt Minion Pro

Printed and bound by CPI Group (UK) Ltd, Croydon, CR0 4YY

ISBN 978 1913208 585

British Library Cataloguing in Publication Data.
A catalogue record for this book is available from the British Library.

To my parents– and Baboon.

PROLOGUE

The rucksack bounced and jingled as Ellie snaked up the mossy path. Inside, Boo the tabby kitten slept like a baby, able to snooze even when she was tossed about like a popcorn kernel. Ellie suddenly sneezed, jolting her cat awake. Boo opened her big green eyes, uncurled her body, and used one of her razor-sharp claws to unzip the top of the pack.

Peeking her brown-and-white head out of the pack's open slit, Boo looked upon a light pink sky. The air was cool and moist. Above her, huge white clouds came apart like pieces of candyfloss. Boo couldn't look away; she was mesmerised by their patterns and the way their movement caused light to fall on the serene lake flanking the trail.

"Good morning, sleepyhead," said Ellie as she paused on the trail for a drink of water. After taking a sip, she dug inside her coat pocket for her phone so she could snap an Instagram-bound selfie with Boo on her shoulder.

Like a metaphorical light bulb, the camera flash caused Boo to remember something from the night before. She'd made a catastrophic mistake, and correcting it would require retracing Ellie's steps – quickly. There wasn't time to explain, so she leapt to the ground and shouted, "Wait here! I'll be back!" before racing down the marshy trail.

ONE

A FATED MEETING

Four months earlier, in a crowded Cambridge animal shelter, Boo awoke in a panic.

She cried out for her mum and siblings, momentarily forgetting where she was. The young cat, not yet three months old, had only been in the shelter for two days, but her siblings had already been adopted. Boo longed for them and the life they'd begun on a serene Lincolnshire farm, where she and her brothers spent hours running through fields, climbing up trees, and playing games beneath the glint of moonlight. Boo was so good at climbing, the owners of the farm named her 'Baboon', or 'Boo' for short (like monkeys, Boo was also clever and mischievous).

The farm had been her empire until several days earlier when the family patriarch used fish-flavoured treats to lure Boo and her brothers into a soft crate. He and his wife drove the confused kittens to the shelter, saying goodbye with tears in their eyes and promises of 'forever homes'.

Boo didn't know what that meant, but she hated this place. She hated its small cages, bright lights, and the lack of grass, bugs, and birds. Most of all, she hated that she was all alone. She lowered her striped head and began to cry as she considered the possibility that she might have to spend the rest of her life in this lonely world of walls and desperate meows.

Suddenly, a friendly face appeared at her cage door. It was a young woman with pink cheeks and green eyes shining with excitement.

The kitten darted to the edge of the cage, jutting her right paw through its metal slats as if to say, *I'm here! Choose me!*

The woman took Boo's paw in her hand, shook it, and said, "Hello, wild-looking cat. I'm Ellie."

Ellie Caldwell was a twenty-two-year-old girl with auburn hair and long, spidery legs who loved animals more than anything in the world. Growing up on a farm in Oxfordshire, she helped her parents care for goats, sheep, and cows, and the family always had pet cats and dogs. Cats were her favourite. She admired their independence and curiosity and appreciated that people have to earn their trust.

Since childhood, Ellie dreamt about working with wild animals in far-off places. Lying in bed at night, her pet cat

purring beside her, she imagined that she was curled up with a pride of lions.

It seemed like a distant fantasy – the sort of thing your parents try to make you let go of – but three weeks after Ellie graduated from the University of Chester with a bachelor of science in conservation biology, she boarded a plane bound for Africa. During her last two years at university, Ellie had spent nearly every weekend volunteering at the Chester Zoo; one time, a senior keeper let Ellie feed the giraffes, but she mostly shovelled hay and scooped up poo. Coupled with good marks and a passionate cover letter, this hands-on experience helped Ellie secure a yearlong job with Namibia's Big Cat Conservancy.

It was there, under the African night sky, that Ellie realised: she *had* to work in wildlife conservation. Nothing else would do. But she didn't have the foundational knowledge required for a full-time career in the field, so she applied to the University of Cambridge's conservation master's programme and made peace with the fact that, if accepted, she'd have to leave Africa and her beloved big cats behind... if only for a while.

Saying goodbye was dreadful, but Ellie was ecstatic (and a little nervous) about studying at Cambridge. However, a week after moving into her Darwin College flat, Ellie felt blue – and incomplete. Before falling asleep each night, she closed her eyes and imagined that she was lying in her tent in Namibia, the air thick with the sound of lion roars. During one of these half-asleep fantasy sessions, a light bulb went off in Ellie's mind: if she couldn't be near her favourite wild cat, she'd adopt a smaller one of her own.

TWO

FINDING A FOREVER HOME

Back at Ellie's student flat at Darwin College, Boo nervously paced and meowed. She had hoped to move back to the countryside – somewhere full of nature and wildlife – but here she was, trapped inside a two-room flat. Thinking direct communication best, Boo voiced her unhappiness with this arrangement.

"Couldn't we find somewhere outside of Cambridge?" she asked Ellie.

Ellie ignored Boo, carrying on with what she called 'cat-proofing' the flat. Perhaps Ellie didn't hear Boo. (She seemed awfully concerned about the placement of the litter tray.)

"Excuse me!" said Boo, much louder this time. "I need to talk to you."

Still, nothing.

Boo leapt towards Ellie, jumping on furniture and running between Ellie's legs, all the while asking if they could please have a chat.

Finally, Ellie responded, "Good gracious, Boo. What's going on with you? I've never heard a cat meow so much!" Ellie dropped down to her knees and stroked Boo's soft ears. "If only you could talk." She chuckled to herself, saying, "A talking cat. Now that would be a scientific discovery!"

When Ellie stood up and walked into the kitchen to make herself a cup of tea, Boo finally realised the problem.

She could understand humans, but when she tried to speak to them, all they heard was, "Meow, meow, meow."

The signs had been there all along.

When she asked the farmers what 'forever homes' meant, they didn't respond. Then, in the shelter, Boo demanded that the veterinarian provide an update on her siblings' whereabouts. Like the farmers, the vet simply looked away.

The realisation that she couldn't communicate with Ellie left Boo feeling rotten. How was she going to convey her unhappiness with this indoor prison? How would she ensure that Ellie understood who she really was – what she liked and disliked, and what she wanted to accomplish in life?

In the midst of this downward spiral, Boo began to giggle at the fact that, despite all of their supposed cleverness, humans don't speak the language of animals.

All of the other animals Boo had met – from eastern grey squirrels to birds and mice – were able to speak to and understand one another. What was it about humans, Boo wondered, that prevented them from understanding animals?

She didn't know, but several hours later Boo had an idea: if Ellie couldn't *hear* her, Boo would *show* the Cambridge student how she felt.

When Ellie went to class the following morning, Boo began leaving coded messages around the flat. Boo leapt around like a lemur and used her long claws to open all of the curtains; this way, Ellie would see her interest in the outside world. Boo left some scratch marks on the curtains during the process but figured a little damage would highlight her frustration.

After a quick snack, Boo moved Ellie's pillows and cushions around to create a perch on the bed.

From there, she looked upon the college gardens, where she could see ducks swimming in the River Cam and squirrels chasing one another up trees. Drawing from her rich imagination, Boo pretended that she was outside with them, playing games like hide-and-seek and king of the castle. One minute, she was tucked under the bed waiting for an imaginary playmate to discover her hiding place; another, she was running around the flat's small kitchen as she imagined mice and robins enjoying a spirited game of chase.

Watching wild animals through the window and pretending she was one of them brought Boo some satisfaction, but her inability to join them outside soon began driving the kitten crazy.

Plus, Ellie wasn't receiving Boo's messages. As smart as Ellie was in the classroom, she sometimes failed to see what was right in front of her. She'd focus on Boo's crazy antics, unable to see the larger problem – that Boo needed space and adventures in nature. Years later, a butterfly told Boo that by focusing on details instead of the big picture, Ellie failed to 'see the forest for the trees'.

Boo's hyperactive behaviour often irritated Ellie, but Ellie never stayed mad for long. One look at the cat's striped face and fluffy white paws and Ellie immediately softened. Secretly, she liked Boo's wild streak because she had one, too.

THREE

THE GREAT OUTDOORS

On a sunny Friday morning several weeks later, Boo watched as Ellie opened a hidden storage space she'd failed to notice during extensive patrols of the flat.

It was too high for Boo to jump into, so she sat on the floor, curiously observing as Ellie stood on her tiptoes and began pulling things down. First came a thick blanket with a zipper on one side. Then an enormous teal rucksack tumbled to the floor. Boo thought it looked like a fun place to hide, so she jumped on it and began exploring its many folds. She found the perfect one for a game of hide-and-seek and slipped inside to see if Ellie would spot her.

"I see you there, Boo. Don't get too comfortable. You're not coming camping with me this weekend."

Boo had other ideas. She didn't know what camping was, but it appeared to involve leaving the flat, and she would do ANYTHING to go outside.

As Ellie rushed around grabbing sweaters and boots, Boo hatched a plan: she'd put on a gloomy face and sit near the front door, dutifully waiting while Ellie made final preparations, behaving as if she were sad to see her go. Then, at the last minute, when Ellie began to reach for her pack, Boo would dive into an open compartment and stash herself away like a stowaway on a ship.

The pack, it turned out, was like a ship, in that its constant movement made Boo feel dizzy, but she knew she had to keep quiet lest Ellie discover her and return her to the flat.

Boo quickly discovered that camping trips began with a bumpy drive and then a long walk up a big hill. The campsite, where the two pitched a tent and slept at night, was at the top of the hill. This was convenient because it meant that Ellie would be so far into her journey when Boo revealed herself, the outdoorsy student wouldn't dare turn back.

Boo found a small hole in the pack from which she could see the world around her. It was full of bright green leaves and views of manicured fields. Boo saw insects buzzing around and heard birds chattering on tree branches. She was so overcome with happiness, she forgot her stowaway status and let out a joyous meow.

Ellie stopped in her tracks.

Knowing that she'd just risked her covert operation, Boo tried to hide beneath a T-shirt in the pocket where she'd hidden herself, but it was no use. Ellie unzipped every one of the pack's compartments and soon found Boo shaking like a leaf.

"What in the world, Boo?!?" She sounded upset. "You can't be up here with me. It isn't safe."

Boo wrinkled her nose, wondering why Ellie would consider the outdoors unsafe for a cat that was born on a farm.

"I grew up outside!" Boo shouted. "This is all I know."

Of course, Ellie just heard meows, and it was clear from the worried look on her face that she wasn't comfortable with Boo being away from the safety of Darwin College.

Luckily, Boo had a bright idea: she needed Ellie to see that she was not only comfortable in this environment, she excelled in it, so she jumped out of the pack and began running up and down the trail. She even climbed a nearby tree, delicately balancing on one of its lofty branches before leaping down like a leopard.

"Fine," Ellie said, her mouth breaking into a subtle smile, "you can camp with me. Just this once."

That night, Boo saw fire for the first time. The campfire blazed red and blue and sent smoke spiralling into the night sky. When burning logs turned to smouldering embers, Ellie yawned and picked Boo up to carry her to the tent – but not before posting an Instagram story in which she called Boo an 'adventure cat'.

Boo, however, wasn't sleepy. (Adventure cats rarely are.)

Cats are most active at dawn and dusk, and Boo was energised from the day's adventure. Sitting by the fire, her ears fully perked, she'd heard mesmerising animal sounds coming from every direction. There was a fox nearby, of that she was certain, and she'd noticed birdcalls she'd never heard before.

So when Ellie fell asleep, Boo tiptoed towards the edge of the tent, used her claws to open its door, and slipped outside.

Boo crept around the campsite, sniffing for animal scents while listening for unfamiliar noises. Just then, the birdcall she'd heard all evening erupted from a cluster of shrubs five yards down the hill. Boo gingerly made her way there, knowing she could injure herself with a misstep or, worse, find herself face to face with a predator. Just because she was confident outside didn't mean she was invincible; her birth mother had taught her all about safety.

Boo reached the shrubs and stopped to give a welcome meow to the birds living inside its dense foliage.

No reply.

The night was so still, Boo wondered if she'd approached the wrong bush, but she could hear a bit of twitching inside, so she meowed again.

"Go away, cat!" said a delicate female voice. "Please leave us alone!"

"I, umm, just wanted to say hi," clarified Boo, taking a few steps backwards. Having heard that cats sometimes hunt birds, she wanted to establish that she wasn't a threat.

"Oh, forgive me," came the small voice as a beautiful pink-breasted dove appeared. "I've never seen a cat before," said the dove.

"I've never seen a bird like you," responded Boo. "What kind are you?"

"We're turtle doves," answered the bird. "We live in West Africa most of the year but migrate to England for the summer. Won't be here much longer, in fact."

Boo inched closer, wanting to hear more, but the dove retreated into the shadows.

"We have to be careful around predators like you," said the dove. "We can't risk anything these days, what with the problems caused by farmers."

"What do you mean?" Boo asked. She thought about the farm where she was born but couldn't imagine it hurting birds.

A turtle dove chick joined its mother, and then the father appeared.

In a deep, commanding voice, he explained the situation: "More and more farms are being created in the area, which means there are fewer plants and trees for us to live in. That's why we moved to the top of this hill."

He pointed his wing towards the valley of neatly crafted farm plots below and sadly proclaimed, "That's where our ancestors used to spend their summers... for centuries... but our historic homes are gone now."

"Increasingly, farmers are also using pesticides," added the mother.

"What's a pestici...?" Boo asked.

"It's a kind of poison – a chemical that keeps insects from eating plants – but it also kills birds and means we can't build our nests anywhere near farms."

Boo felt overwhelmed. She wondered if her birthplace used poison on its crops; she also thought about cats like her mum who spent their entire lives outside. Were they at risk, too?

"The good news," continued the male dove, "is that some farmers have stopped using pesticides. A friend of ours said that where he lives, which is about twenty kilometres from here, all the plants are poison-free, and farmers are also replanting the shrubs and trees we need to survive."

"So, we just need to get all the farmers to do the same thing?" asked Boo, not realising that she'd said 'we' when considering who could persuade farmers to change their practices.

"I suppose," said the mother dove, "but I don't know how. We can't talk to people. We can whistle and sing and tap on their windows, but they don't understand us."

"Can you talk to people?" asked the turtle dove chick, her eyes as wide as the moon above.

"No," said Boo, lowering her gaze to the ground. "I don't think any animals can."

Just then, a loud howl came from the top of the ridge. At first, Boo thought it was a fox, but it didn't take long for her to realise that the desperate call was coming from Ellie's mouth – and it was meant for Boo.

"I have to go," stammered Boo as she sprinted up the hill. "My mum is going to kill me!"

Boo raced up the hill with lightning speed, her tail helping her balance as she charged across uneven ground.

By the time she reached the hilltop, Ellie's screeching had ceased, but her bright red cheeks told Boo that she was anything but relaxed.

Boo brushed up against Ellie's legs and turned her big green eyes upwards. She took a deep breath and once again attempted to verbally communicate with Ellie. Deep down, Boo knew it was futile, but she needed Ellie to hear her words now more than ever.

"I met some turtle doves, and they're in trouble because of farmers," said Boo. "We have to help them!"

Ellie looked down at Boo, her angry face softening.

Hurray, thought Boo, *it's finally working!*

"How can I stay angry at that face?" Ellie said, lifting Boo into her arms.

After they'd returned to their sleeping positions, Boo nestled in the crook of Ellie's elbow, the kitten wondered aloud, "Just the other day, I heard you say that conservation happens in the wild, and not in a classroom, and here's a chance to actually do something."

Boo suddenly felt upset – like the problem belonged to her and not just the doves living on the hillside.

Yawning, Ellie wished Boo a good night and gently drifted back to sleep.

FOUR

A BREAKTHROUGH

Ellie was so tired from the commotion of the night before, she slept through a spectacular sunrise. Boo had been awake for hours and let herself out of the tent in time to witness the sky's changing hues. From black to lavender, then pink to orange; she'd enjoyed many dawns on the farm, but she'd never been high up enough to see a sunrise as glorious as today's.

When Ellie finally emerged, a groggy-eyed mess, Boo purred as loudly as a fully-grown cheetah and jumped into Ellie's arms to give her cuddles and kisses.

"I get it, Boo," said Ellie as she gently scratched Boo's chin. "You're sorry."

Boo was elated to discover that Ellie understood her frame of mind – at least this once. Little did she know, the moment marked a new chapter for the duo, one in which Ellie began to pick up on Boo's feelings and moods.

From that moment on, their nonverbal communication grew and grew. Several weeks later, on a gloomy Friday night, Ellie appeared to understand one of Boo's complex thoughts for the first time. They were sitting together on Ellie's small beige sofa, Boo purring away as Ellie typed up her first graded essay. It was on the subject of small-scale British farming – whether it positively or negatively impacts people and the environment.

Ellie crafted a sentence and read it aloud: "Local, small-scale farmers provide healthy farm-to-table food to the British people."

Boo felt the sharp pang of hunger. She'd already had dinner but could go for a snack. Some cheese, perhaps? As she thought about food, Boo remembered something the male turtle dove said weeks earlier. *More and more farms are being created in the area, which means there are fewer plants and trees for us to live in.*

Ellie was so focused on how farms help people that she completely forgot to consider how they negatively impact wild birds.

Boo jumped up, landing with a crash on Ellie's laptop.

"Well, excuse me, Boo," said Ellie, gently guiding Boo back to her favourite spot on the sofa before carrying on typing.

"Wait!" Boo shouted, her words coming out in meows. "You're forgetting something, and it's REALLY IMPORTANT!"

Ellie stopped typing and slowly rotated her face towards Boo. She had a strange look in her eyes – like she'd seen a ghost. A friendly one.

"What was that, Boo?" she asked.

Boo locked eyes with Ellie and concentrated as she carefully repeated the dove's words.

Ellie's curved lips opened a little, and she started vigorously nodding. Then she lifted her fingers from the keyboard and began to crack her knuckles while talking to herself: "Of course, native trees are often the first to get cut down."

She tossed her laptop aside, hopped up from the sofa, and sprinted towards the small wooden bookshelf in her bedroom. She began pulling books out – one after another – until she returned with one in hand. The title was *Land Use and Wildlife*, and it looked really old. The spine was cracking and there was a stain on the front cover. Boo hadn't noticed this book before and it seemed like Ellie hadn't either.

Boo was about to remark on this fact when Ellie dropped the book to the ground and began squealing like a wild animal. "Hold the phone!" she said. Ellie lifted her hands to her mouth, covering it as her eyes grew as wide as a full moon.

Boo was perplexed: she wasn't holding anything and certainly didn't have a phone in her paws.

"Excuse me?" Boo asked.

"You can talk!" exclaimed Ellie. "And I can understand you?"

"It appears that way," said Boo with a giggle. "We're talking right now, aren't we?"

"This is crazy," continued Ellie. "I've been around animals since the day I was born, and I've never, ever heard one speak. I mean, horses have communicative facial expressions, and dogs seem to know your mood before you do, but talking? Like this? No, no, no. This can't be real."

Ellie plopped onto the sofa before staring at Boo with wonder in her eyes. She opened her mouth to speak, but no words emerged.

"I suppose this must be strange for you," offered Boo. "To be fair, no human has ever understood me or any of my animal friends, but we're able to talk to one another. On the farm where I grew up—"

"You grew up on a farm?" Ellie asked incredulously.

"Yes, in Lincolnshire, but anyway, I was saying." Without meaning to, Boo had begun speaking very rapidly. "Ever since I learnt to talk, I've been able to converse with every kind of animal, from squirrels to birds to dogs to sheep."

"But, how?" Ellie asked. Her brain couldn't process this information. It didn't make sense; there was no scientific backing for it. Ellie would know.

"I don't know *how*," said Boo. "I've never asked anyone how it works, and no one's ever asked me. It just... is. I assumed I could communicate with humans, too, but I've been trying to talk to you for weeks to no avail. I nearly gave up, but at the end of our camping trip it seemed like something shifted."

"What do you mean?"

"First, you started to understand my moods. Then, a few days ago, you seemed to get the gist of what I was saying. Prior to that, when I spoke out loud, you just heard meows, but suddenly, you understood me, if only a little."

"Okay," said Ellie as she fiddled with her hair, "that seems to add up."

"And here we are today – having a full-blown conversation!" responded Boo.

Boo tiptoed across the sofa to Ellie, whose face had lost most of its colour, and lovingly folded into her lap.

"Isn't it wonderful?" she said, purring.

"It's the most," Ellie paused to take a deep breath, "incredible thing in the world."

They sat quietly, purring and smiling, as they contemplated the magnitude of this moment. Although Boo had spent weeks desperately pursuing this breakthrough, she never thought it would actually happen. Ellie, meanwhile, never considered that she'd be able to verbally communicate with animals, so her mind was a storm of emotions and ideas.

"Do you think I could research this? And write about it?" asked Ellie after several silent minutes.

Boo hadn't thought about the fact that Ellie might want to tell the world about their bond and what it could mean for animal–human relationships generally. Boo didn't know why, but she felt sick to her stomach as she mulled over the implications of research and publicity.

"I, well, I don't know," she said morosely. "I think I like the fact that this two-way communication is ours and ours alone."

Ellie nodded. "Our little secret?"

"Yes," responded Boo, "at least for now…"

Ellie looked at her watch and realised an hour had passed since she grabbed *Land Use and Wildlife* from her bookshelf. As distracted as she was by her newfound ability to understand Boo, she had to finish her essay. Not handing it in could mean failing out of her conservation master's programme.

"Boo, my darling, we need to put a pin in this."

"A pin?" Boo was confused.

"It's a matter of speech. We need to revisit this subject later, because I have to finish this essay, and to do that, I need to read this dull-looking book!"

She pointed to it and cleared her throat, which was a very British way of telling Boo to move back to her spot on the other side of the sofa.

As Ellie skimmed several chapters, occasionally reading passages aloud, Boo's mind ran wild with emotions and ideas. Knowing that she and Ellie could finally communicate on a deep level brought Boo a sense of unparalleled satisfaction; going forward, Ellie would understand Boo's feelings and desires, which meant the two could enjoy a meaningful, two-sided friendship.

With Ellie focused on her book and Boo lost in happy thoughts, both cat and human failed to see one of the most powerful things about their ability to converse: they could work together to help endangered animals. They didn't realise it that evening, but Boo would go on to become a translator of sorts: an intermediary between wild animals and the people protecting them.

FIVE

SOCIAL MEDIA

After Ellie handed in her essay, she spent a night on the town celebrating with her classmates. Boo, meanwhile, sat at home staring out the bedroom window into the darkness beyond. It was awfully dark for early evening, leaving Boo with a pang of longing for summertime… the endless days, warm air, and beautiful flowers. Boo remembered her mother teaching her and her siblings about the changing of the seasons, but her mum definitely skipped the part about autumn's dark and dismal days.

Ellie wasn't home by midnight or one or two, and Boo began to worry that Ellie might never return.

Perhaps she could go out searching for her, thereby escaping the confines of the flat... if only she knew where to look. For a moment, Boo's anxiety morphed into excitement, but she quickly remembered why she was thinking about leaving the flat in the first place and regained her focus.

Boo pounced onto the small dining table where Ellie did most of her studying, inadvertently knocking a pile of papers onto the floor. She put them back in place and opened Ellie's laptop, its strange glow illuminating her whiskers like moonlight on water. If there were clues about Ellie's whereabouts, the laptop's calendar would hold them.

But the calendar held no clues. Its only entry for the day – 11th October 2019 – read, *4:00pm: essay due.* However, there was an email open on Ellie's screen from someone called Claire, whom Boo immediately recognised as one of Ellie's classmates and friends. The subject line was *Celebratory Drinks*, and the body of the email mentioned a place called The Eagle. This, Boo realised, must be an invitation to celebrate handing in the essay Ellie had spent weeks writing.

Her worries misplaced, Boo returned to feeling bored, and Ellie's laptop seemed the perfect distraction. It had folders and pictures and tabs galore. Like most little kids, Boo wasn't allowed screen time, so she seized the opportunity to sneak some in.

Boo tapped one of her claws on a colourful circle, which caused a flurry of webpages to open. The first to appear was Instagram.

Boo hissed. She hated Instagram.

Besides school, Instagram was the only thing that regularly diverted Ellie's attention away from Boo. Often, when the two were enjoying quality time together, Ellie grabbed her phone and began furiously typing before proudly announcing that she'd posted another #catstagram of her and Boo. On their camping trip, Ellie kept making Boo sit still on her shoulder as she snapped selfies of the two of them. Sensing Boo's irritation, Ellie had explained that Instagram isn't just about followers and likes; it's a powerful tool for communicating things that matter, like wildlife conservation, but Boo wasn't convinced. To her, it seemed like a waste of time.

However, given this rare opportunity to play with Ellie's favourite toy (her laptop), Boo decided to spend some time on Instagram to see what all the fuss was about. She scrolled through Ellie's page and couldn't help smiling when she saw photos of her with her best friend. Their pictures were cute, and they seemed to attract a lot of attention from people who liked animals and nature.

Boo quickly observed that Ellie's feed also included beautiful images of places Ellie had visited, like Namibia. There were cute pictures of lion cubs and captions about conservation and sustainability. Ellie also regularly shared photos and videos from her time volunteering at Chester Zoo, and the zoo often reposted her stories. Most surprising, however, was the sheer number of people following Ellie. There were ten thousand of them! How can anyone know ten thousand people? Or even a hundred people? Boo counted the number of humans she'd met: it was a whopping eleven.

How did Ellie achieve so much success in this virtual world? Boo wondered. Were her photographs *that* special? Were her stories *that* good?

It was late, said the tiny computer clock, and Boo finally felt sleepy, but she couldn't resist trying her paw at Instagram. After all, this could be her only chance.

She flipped on the living room lights and repositioned herself in front of the computer screen, careful to give her friendliest smile before letting the camera snap away. It took a bit of googling and trial-and-error, but Boo figured out how to upload a photo along with a caption. She decided to keep it short and sweet: *Home alone. #catlife #catselfie #catstagram #boothecat*

Suddenly, a door opened and slammed shut. Ellie was home (FINALLY), and Boo was still at the computer. She gasped, knowing she'd been caught red-handed (or, if we're getting technical, red-pawed).

Boo turned to face Ellie while attempting to close the laptop with her tail, but it was no use. Tails don't work like that. Besides, Ellie could see the glowing laptop screen from where she stood.

Boo lowered her head in shame – she knew better than to sneak onto Ellie's computer and publish posts on her behalf – but was pleasantly surprised to see a smile emerging on Ellie's face.

"Instagram, eh?" said Ellie with a chuckle. "I thought you hated it when I went online."

"Well, I, umm," said Boo, a little nervously, "that's sort of true. I don't like it when you turn your attention away from me and towards your phone or computer, but I may have misjudged social media."

"Is that right?" asked Ellie as she scooped Boo into her arms.

"I didn't realise you were talking about conservation on Instagram," said Boo. "I thought it was just a platform where people show off how wonderful they and their lives are."

"To be fair, for many people it is," continued Ellie, "but not for me. I use social media to interact with fellow wildlife-lovers all over the world. We share pictures of animals and discuss ways to help endangered species. Of course, you're on there, too."

"I saw," said a smiling Boo.

"You're my adventure cat," continued Ellie as the two got cosy in bed. "My camping, hiking, animal-loving adventure cat. And," she continued, "we have a new adventure on the horizon."

Boo opened her half-closed eyes and excitedly asked, "A camping trip?"

"Indeed. To Norfolk next weekend."

This was music to Boo's fluffy ears! She had spent weeks dreaming about this day, but with Ellie spending more and more time studying, she'd started to give up hope.

But wait: can you go camping when it's cold outside?

"There's just one condition," Ellie stated, "no running off in the middle of the night. This time, you're sticking with me."

Boo nodded politely even though she had no intention of spending the midnight hour – her favourite time of day – in a tent with a human when new animal friends were in her midst. *No*, thought Boo, *I'll find a way to sneak out.* After all, she'd done it before…

SIX

THE NORFOLK BROADS

Boo was so excited about camping, she could barely sleep. She was like a child on the eve of Christmas whose anticipation causes insomnia. But she must have drifted off to sleep at some point, for when Ellie pulled back her green duvet and stepped out of bed, Boo found herself jolted awake from a vivid dream. The dream was foggy now and fading into grainy particles, but as Boo sat up in bed, she could see one image clearly: a beautiful building surrounded by thousands of people and animals. There were badgers everywhere, and they were holding microphones and signs. Boo and Ellie were there, too, and they appeared to be chanting something to the crowds…

"Wakey, wakey," said Ellie as she appeared in the doorway balancing a cup of tea in one hand and her rucksack in the other. "We need to get a move on, my dear. Norfolk awaits."

Boo twirled out of bed, ran circles around the room, and responded, "I'm ready. I was born ready!"

They emerged from Darwin College to a crisp November day; the skies were as clear as ice and leaves rustled in the wind, making a delightful sound.

Boo assumed that she and Ellie were driving to Norfolk, but Ellie had other ideas. She'd been vowing to use her car less since public transport is often better for the environment, so Boo was about to have her first train experience.

The train carriage was crowded, so Boo had to spend the first half hour beneath Ellie's seat squashed against the sides of her carrier. She hated missing out on the action all around her, and the floor smelt funny, but when the carriage cleared out several stops later, Ellie let Boo sit in her lap so the kitten could look out the window.

Fields of heather flashed by. Above them, grey clouds ate up the sky, blocking what little light the British sun offered this time of year. Crows perched on treetops and telephone wires, their gazes fixed on the ground below as if something incredible were about to happen. *It's beautiful*, thought Boo, *all of it*. More than anything, the kitten loved seeing a new place. Travelling, she realised, was a great adventure. She wanted to do more of it, though her favourite method of exploration was on foot.

An hour later, as the duo began hiking through the Herringfleet Hills, Boo got to feel the soft earth under her paws once more. She was happy, at peace, joy splashed across her face. Until now, Boo had nothing but bad things to say about autumn's dark hours and cold temperatures, but out in the elements, where she felt and heard and smelt its crispness, Boo realised that autumn had its own appeal. The leaves were vibrant colours – reds, oranges, and yellows – and they spiralled from the trees in mesmerising swirls.

Norfolk was nothing like Lincolnshire or Cambridge. For one thing, it was near an ocean, which Ellie described as a giant pool of water. Boo hated water, so she was glad they weren't going near it on their weekend trip, but Ellie quickly dismantled Boo's relief.

"I hate to tell you, little one, but water is in our future."

Just then, they rounded a bend, and Boo spotted the unmistakable shimmer of water. Boo had never seen so much water – it was all around them. Fear danced up her spine, causing Boo to jump onto Ellie's rucksack and slide into one of its open pockets where she became, for the first time in her life, a genuine scaredy-cat.

"Relax, Boo," said Ellie gently. "We're not going *in* the water! These lakes, or broads as they're known in England, aren't deep anyway. But we'll be on land – safe and sound and plenty dry for your sensitive kitty cat paws."

After a long hike, during which Boo spent a good hour on her own four feet, Ellie announced that they were setting up camp. It was only 4pm, far earlier than when they stopped exploring last time.

Boo protested, "Why are we stopping? There's still so much more time before dinner!"

"The sun is nearly gone," said Ellie, pointing towards a rose-coloured horizon. "We have to set up camp before it gets completely dark, but if you're well-behaved this evening, we can go for a short walk after dinner."

Boo knew better; people aren't very good at doing things in the dark. Whenever Ellie needed to find something – say, one of the stakes for the tent or her metal water bottle – she used a bright light on her phone. Boo could see everything clearly, and the light merely bothered her, but Ellie, it seemed, needed assistance.

Darkness also made Ellie sleepy. She always started yawning the second the sun went down. Tonight, as soon as dinner was over, Ellie's eyelids began to droop as she yawned time and again.

"It's not bedtime yet! You promised me a walk!" squealed Boo, eager to see more of this new place – even if it was full of lakes and streams.

But it was too late; Ellie was half-asleep on top of her sleeping bag.

Boo curled up next to Ellie, feeling the warmth of her body. The comfort she felt when pressed against Ellie made Boo feel safe – like nothing could hurt her. She'd never be the terrified cat alone in a shelter again. She had Ellie, and Ellie had her.

But as Boo lay there purring contentedly, she couldn't help imagining the world beyond the tent. She wanted to explore it – had to – but she also felt guilty about the fact that, by doing so, she'd go against Ellie's wishes. It was an ethical dilemma without an easy solution, but an instinct deep in Boo's gut insisted she go out on her own… Something, or someone, needed her.

Having made a quiet escape, Boo got her bearings. She listened, looked, and sniffed while standing still, thinking something would guide her. A sign. But she didn't pick up anything out of the ordinary, so she decided to walk up the trail.

Uncharacteristically, Boo moved slowly, fearing that a swift motion in the Norfolk Broads could land her in a pool of water. She used her whiskers to navigate tight spots and holes in the ground.

She was whisker-deep in one such hole when a deep voice startled her.

"Who's there?" rumbled a heavy, scratchy male voice. "And what do you want?"

Boo tried to wriggle her head out of the hole, but she was stuck, so she called back, "It's me, umm, Boo."

"Boo? Who?"

"A cat, just a cat. I'm here camping," Boo stammered, feeling embarrassed and a little scared. Maybe she should have stayed in the tent after all.

She continued trying to wriggle her face out of the hole, but it was no use. She was officially stuck. Boo heard footsteps. She squinted her eyes, trying to make out the form approaching from deep in the hole, but it was too dark. Even with feline night vision, she couldn't see a thing.

"It's just a kitten!" howled the voice, now close. "I'm Boris. I live in this den with my family."

As Boris inched closer, Boo could see black-and-white stripes adorning his face.

"What are you, Boris?"

Before he answered, a soft snout touched Boo's nose, nudging her backwards and out of the hole. She landed on her bum with a loud thump and sat on the den's rim, blinking.

"A badger," said Boris as he waddled Boo's way and joined her outside the den. "European," he continued in what sounded like a French accent, "but I'm English through-and-through. Good thing Brexit won't apply to animals!" He roared with laughter. "Bonnie!" he shouted into his cavernous home. "Come meet this cat! She's harmless!"

A female badger soon appeared, extending her paw towards Boo for a rather formal greeting. She, Boris, and Boo sat on the ground a bit awkwardly – each of them waiting for the other to say something.

Finally, Boo got the courage to speak: "I'm so sorry I disturbed you. I was just out exploring the Broads. I live in Cambridge in a flat with a conservation student named Ellie."

"A who, what?" asked Bonnie.

"She's a human, and she's studying conservation."

"What's that?" asked Boris.

"It's a type of science that involves helping wild animals and nature. Actually, you might find this interest—"

Boo was about to ask them if they knew any farmers when Boris clasped his front paws together and began speaking rapidly. "My goodness, that's a coincidence!" he said. "We've been talking to our friends and family about this very thing… conservation, you call it?"

Boo nodded.

"We have friends in Devon who have sent us messages about culls taking place near their home."

Boo looked confused. "What's a cull?" she asked.

The two badgers looked at each other for a moment; they seemed nervous about answering Boo's question.

Bonnie finally said, "It's an awful thing. It's when people kill a number of animals to satisfy a particular goal. In this case, people say that we badgers pass diseases to cattle, so they want to get rid of us."

Bonnie sounds regal, thought Boo, *like a queen… but a morose one.*

"It's absolute nonsense," added Boris. "They can simply vaccinate us against the disease, which would prevent us from getting ill in the first place, but they seem to think it's easier to shoot us instead." His eyes were gleaming red, and he was huffing and puffing.

"Calm down, dear," said Bonnie, giving him a gentle pat on the back.

"Anyway," she continued, her eyes turning back to Boo, "we're terribly worried about our friends and have reason to believe that future culls may include other areas, including Norfolk, so we're terrified as well. We don't know what to do. We've tried everything, but we can't seem to make any difference on our own. We need to find people who can help us."

Bonnie glanced up at Boo with a glint in her eye.

Boo looked at Bonnie, then Boris, a smile overtaking her face. "I think," she said confidently, "I may be able to help."

Boris and Bonnie couldn't stop beaming as Boo told them about Ellie, and neither could Boo. She was delighted by the fact that she could offer a glimmer of hope during these dark times, and she couldn't wait to introduce her wild animal friends to Ellie. Fortunately, the badger family had access to a phone, which guaranteed ongoing communication and completely shocked Boo – if country badgers had phones, surely Boo could get one?

Boris had Boo write down Ellie's mobile number on a slip of paper and said he and Bonnie would phone in a week's time. They were heading out on a family vacation early the following morning and would be offline until their return.

"Got to unplug," said Boris with a wink.

Boo said farewell and bounded up the trail.

When Boo returned to the tent, she was absolutely knackered; she fell asleep before brushing her teeth and was sleeping like a log when Ellie stirred at 6am. Ellie wanted to get an early start to ensure she and Boo had a full day in the Broads before heading back to Cambridge, so she packed up their things while Boo carried on dozing.

By 7am, she was ready to go, but Boo was still fast asleep. Ellie decided to let the kitten continue resting, so she carefully placed her at the top of the pack, zipped it up to make sure Boo stayed warm, and struck out on the trail.

"Achoo!" Ellie sneezed a half hour later.

Boo jolted awake, but it was awfully dark. Where was she? It took a few seconds (and a giant yawn) to get her bearings: she was sleeping on a pile of clothes in Ellie's rucksack, as she sometimes did when outdoor adventures zapped her energy. Boo used one of her razor-sharp claws to unzip the clothes-filled pouch.

Peeking her head out of the pack's open slit, Boo looked upon a light pink sky. The air was crisp. Above her, misshapen clouds came apart like pieces of candyfloss. Boo couldn't look away; she was mesmerised by their patterns and the way their movement caused light to fall on the small lake beside the trail.

"Good morning, sleepyhead," said Ellie as she paused on the trail for a drink of water. After taking a sip, she dug inside her coat pocket for her phone so she could take an Instagram-bound selfie with Boo on her shoulder.

Like a metaphorical light bulb, the camera flash caused Boo to remember something from the night before. In her sleepy state, she had given Bonnie and Boris Ellie's old phone number – the one Ellie recently discarded along with her previous phone, which never worked. Boo had no idea what time it was, but she knew the badgers were leaving early for their family trip, and if they left the area without Ellie's new number, they wouldn't be able to get in touch.

Her grogginess gone, Boo knew what she had to do: she'd have to retrace Ellie's steps – and quickly! There wasn't time to explain her abrupt departure, so she leapt to the ground and shouted, "Wait here! I'll be back!" before racing down the marshy trail.

Every step kicked up bits of sticky mud, so Boo looked more like a rat than a cat when she reached Boris and Bonnie's den.

"Helloooooo!" she shouted from its edge. "Boris! Bonnie! It's Boo!"

She cocked her ears to listen.

But besides the unmistakeable sound of buzzing insects, Boo heard nothing. *If only I'd brought a pen and paper*, she thought to herself. Then she could leave a note with Ellie's new number.

Boo felt wretched as she considered her mistake. She was embarrassed and angry with herself, and as if the phone number mix-up wasn't bad enough, Ellie would be furious with Boo when she returned. This was only their second overnight adventure; Boo was still proving to Ellie that she was cautious in the wild and respectful of Ellie's rules.

Boo was sitting on the ground feeling cold, muddy, and miserable when she heard a faint whistling sound.

Her chin lifted, and her ears stood at attention. The whistling got louder... and louder... and it was soon joined by a booming voice.

"It'll only take a minute!" the voice said.

Boo recognised the voice: it was Boris! She was so excited by his presence, she jumped into the air, twirling her tail.

"Boris!" she squealed. "Where are you, Boris?"

His striped face poked through a dense patch of grass.

"Boo?" he said. "What are you doing here?"

Boo ran up to him, kissed him on the cheek, and began purring uncontrollably.

"I'm so relieved you're here," she said with a huge smile on her face. "I realised this morning that I gave you the wrong phone number last night, and I was so worried that you'd leave home with the wrong one, and we'd never be in touch, and then Ellie and I couldn't help you, and the cull would happen, and—"

"Slow down, little one," Boris said gently. "Take a breath."

Boo inhaled deeply. "Oh, gosh, you're right," she said. "I'm all worked up. Anyway, I ran back to give you the correct phone number. It's 07482—"

"Let me get my notepad, dear," said Boris. Once he had it in hand, Boo repeated the number three times (she wasn't taking any chances!). She gave Boris a huge hug and took off running towards the spot where she'd left Ellie.

SEVEN

#SHAREDPASSION

Unsurprisingly, Ellie was very displeased with Boo when she returned a mess of mud, sweat, and exasperation. She demanded an explanation straight away.

With the speed of the world's fastest express train, Boo told Ellie about meeting the European turtle doves and Bonnie and Boris. Ellie tried to interject to scold Boo for sneaking out, but Boo was so focused, she wouldn't let Ellie get a word in edgeways. She told Ellie about the badger cull and how it would impact her friends, and she begged Ellie to develop a strategy for stopping the cull in its tracks.

Ellie nodded throughout Boo's speech and was visibly surprised when she heard about the cull, but when Boo finished, Ellie stood still, quietly thinking. Boo could practically see the wheels turning inside Ellie's brain.

"Well?" Boo stammered, impatience getting the best of her. "What are we going to do?"

Ellie looked down at Boo and said, "I need some time to think. Let's enjoy our day in the countryside and resume this conversation on the train."

As they carried on walking through the idyllic Broads, Boo continued thinking about Boris and Bonnie. What if she worked with them and other wild animals to help protect endangered wildlife? The idea was exhilarating, but even when Boo pictured a group of animals banding together, she couldn't imagine a world in which non-human animals had the ability to influence powerful people and governments. *Animals are like children*, thought Boo. *No one takes them seriously.*

Ever since she was a wee kitten exploring the fields of Lincolnshire, Boo felt confident. Powerful, even. She was strong and adventurous and good at communicating with other animals (and, more recently, Ellie), but Boo also knew that the world isn't fair. Just because you have a good idea or unique skills doesn't necessarily mean your goals are within reach. Success isn't entirely up to you, and bad things sometimes happen to the best animals and people. Boo learnt this lesson the hard way when she became separated from her mother and siblings at such a young age.

Ellie, on the other hand, possessed an optimistic attitude that Boo found a bit perplexing. When Boo complained about living in a small student flat, Ellie responded with annoying statements like, *Look on the bright side, Boo, the glass is half-full, not half-empty.* And once, when Boo begged Ellie to make pancakes, Ellie claimed that she could make them 'from scratch' without following a recipe. Boo and her taste buds begged to differ. Also, whenever Boo knocked over water glasses, as cats are wont to do, they were definitely half, and then completely, empty.

That Sunday afternoon, as they settled into seats on the train from Norfolk to Cambridge, Boo had an epiphany. Combined, her and Ellie's unique philosophies make an interesting and potentially powerful combination. Boo is a realist who takes a wide view: she has reasonable expectations and always thinks about the big picture. Ellie, on the other hand, is a detail-obsessed optimist. She always sees the best in people and situations, which is charming but can create problems. She keeps moving forwards even when the odds are against her, but is prone to losing her head in the clouds (or, more often than not, the library). Plus, she is so detail-orientated, she sometimes misses the big picture.

On the other hand, Boo and Ellie have a great deal in common: they both love nature, animals, and exploring. And both cat and human believe in the conservation movement's ability to save endangered animals while helping people remember that they are *part* of nature, not *separate* from it.

Ellie was staring out the window as if the field beyond was the most interesting thing she'd ever seen when Boo tried to bring her attention back to their morning conversation.

"Ellie!" Boo shrieked from across the small table separating their seats on the train.

But Ellie kept her eyes fixed on rolling fields of green.

Classic, thought Boo. "Ellie!" she said loudly. "Can we talk about the badger cull, please?"

Ellie looked up and smiled. "Sorry, Boo. I just love riding on trains. It's amazing how you're able to watch landscapes change over mere minutes."

"Yeah, sure, I agree," said Boo. "But what are your thoughts on the cull and actions we can take to stop it?"

"I don't know for sure, Boo, but I have an idea. Why don't we start posting about the cull on social media? I have pictures of badgers from a few years ago, including several of badger cubs that are so cute, they'll definitely get reposted."

A wave of excitement coursed through Boo's body. Not only was Ellie's idea creative, it might actually work.

Boo interjected an idea of her own: "We need memorable hashtags!"

Ellie nodded in agreement.

"How about #killthecull and #badgerlove?"

"Yes and yes," said Ellie. "Together, we can do this."

"Together," Boo corrected, "we can do ANYTHING!"

EIGHT

CLASSES FIT FOR A CAT

As it turned out, Ellie believed that accomplishing anything required accomplishing a lot of little things. First up? Ellie wanted to start sneaking Boo into some of her lectures since Boo knew very little about conservation biology and practice. When she told Boo about her scheme, Boo was so excited, she literally bounced off the walls.

(Well, sort of. Boo jumped onto the kitchen counter but lost her footing, which sent her tumbling to the floor. While clumsily careening downward, one of Boo's back paws touched a wall. That counts, right?)

For a cat intent on exploring new places, going to class every few days sounded downright dreamy, but

Boo quickly discovered that her and Ellie's educational outings were anything but adventurous. For one thing, Ellie couldn't take Boo to class in her cat carrier. It would be much too obvious. Even Ellie's rucksack would raise eyebrows. Why would a master's student suddenly start carrying a camping pack to class?

There was only one solution, and Boo didn't like it: she had to squeeze into Ellie's smaller backpack, the kind students use, to ensure Boo made it to class undetected. Once there, she could open up the backpack and sit on top of it under Ellie's seat, but Boo could barely hear the professors, and she obviously couldn't ask questions.

Nevertheless, Boo found most of Ellie's lectures interesting, and within several weeks of attending classes, she realised that she was well on her way to becoming a real-life conservationist.

Interestingly, just as Boo and Ellie's personalities complemented each other, their conservation interests did, too. Scientific subjects fascinated Ellie. She loved learning about ecology (how plants and animals interact

with their environments) and taxonomy (how different species are related). Boo found these topics so boring, she yawned through every lecture on them and once fell asleep beneath the table, waking up a few minutes later to the sound of her own snoring (side note: Boo snores).

Boo wasn't into hard science; she much preferred learning about animal behaviour. Why, for instance, do lions rub their cheeks against one another? It's not just a friendly greeting, explained one of Boo's favourite professors, lions 'bunt' to communicate and scent-mark. Boo later recognised that whenever she butted her head against Ellie, she was doing the exact same thing!

One afternoon, as Ellie and Boo enjoyed afternoon tea at Ellie's small dining table, Boo had a realisation. If she and Ellie both regularly posted on social media, their distinct interests would lead to the two of them covering more subjects and informing more people. Ellie was open to the suggestion, though she wasn't about to give Boo her own smartphone, so they agreed on an arrangement whereby Boo had one hour a day to use Ellie's phone or laptop – and for conservation purposes only (on that, Ellie was VERY clear). Despite her dedication to social media, Ellie strongly believed that the best things in life happen spontaneously and without technology.

Boo couldn't agree more. She'd gotten comfortable reading articles on Ellie's laptop and occasionally posting on Instagram, but the moment she stepped away, she felt a wave of relief. Her head felt clear and calm, and she was always ready to walk away from technology's unnatural light since it reminded Boo of the horrible shelter where Ellie adopted her.

That evening, Boo developed several social media posts completely on her own, and they were far more dynamic than the one-line #catstagram she'd posted earlier that month. She uploaded one of Ellie's badger pictures, pairing it with a long caption that directly addressed the cull. Boo mentioned Bonnie and Boris and invited social media users to share their reactions to the cull in the comments.

When Ellie and Boo tucked into bed several hours later, Ellie checked her phone one last time before turning off the lamp.

She gasped aloud.

"Oh my God, Boo," she said, jolting upright.

Boo assumed she was in trouble; maybe her post was too political.

"Your Instagram post has fifty comments, and eighty-seven people just started following me."

Boo grinned. "Is that a lot?"

"Yes!" Ellie answered. "I've never had such a powerful reaction to a single post. I wonder if it's because of the cute badger pic. Let me read the comments to see what people are saying."

Boo crawled up Ellie's arm, positioned herself on Ellie's right shoulder, and peered down so she could read the comments, too.

The first one read:

I can't believe the UK government is planning another badger cull. A year ago, my MP promised that badger culls were a thing of the past.

And then:

Badgers are such fascinating creatures. A family lives near my house, and I love watching them interact. England should protect them as national treasures.

The final comment included a wonderful surprise:

Eloise here. I think I know the Boris to whom you refer. Lives in Norfolk? He's my second cousin. Great chap. I know a lot about the cull and have plenty of friends and family members ready to stand up to the government. Give me a shout if you're ever in the Cotswolds.

Ellie and Boo locked eyes.

"These are really thoughtful comments," said Ellie.

"And one is from a badger!" responded Boo.

"I had no idea other animals used social media. I wonder how a wild badger got a social media account?" wondered Ellie.

"Who cares!" responded Boo. "It's amazing that she's not only on Instagram but also engaging with our content. We have to meet her. She could provide us with invaluable information about the cull."

"Guess what, Boo?" said Ellie coyly. "It's your lucky day. The Cotswolds, where Eloise lives, is very close to where I grew up in Oxfordshire, so when we spend Christmas with my parents, we can arrange to meet her."

"That is fabulous news!" said Boo. "Remind me, when are we going to your parents' house?"

"In just under two weeks," answered Ellie. "I cannot wait. Mum makes the most delicious Christmas dinner, and Dad is the master of gift-giving. I swear, he's able to know what you want before you do. This one time…" Ellie trailed off, her smile receding.

"What is it?" asked Boo. "Did Grandpa give you an awful gift?"

"It's not that," continued Ellie. "I got so excited thinking about Christmas with Mum and Dad, I momentarily forgot how much work I have to do over the holidays. We just got an email from our course director saying that, to ensure we complete next term's project on time, we should start our research over the break."

"Why is it called a break, then?" asked a perplexed Boo.

"Great question," said a depressed-sounding Ellie.

She was crestfallen. It was obvious that she wanted to join Boo on one of her wildlife adventures, but she couldn't put her studies aside.

"We'll see," said Boo before giving Ellie a big hug. "I'll understand if you can't come with me to meet Eloise," she added.

After Ellie switched off the bedside lamp, Boo remained awake. She looked out the window, using her supreme vision to make out movements in the trees. Boo could just perceive a grey squirrel running between two branches. Boo thought of Boris and Bonnie, the European turtle doves, and her mum and siblings. She felt something she couldn't quite explain. It was a mix of emotions: happiness, sadness, warmth, and pride. She loved Ellie and enjoyed the limited interactions she'd had with other people, but there was something unique about befriending and communicating with animals.

Animals don't have the same advantages people do. They don't get to attend fancy universities like Cambridge, nor do they have the luxury of spending a gap year in Africa. And because people run the world, the interests of animals are often overlooked. The cull perfectly reflects this: badgers and their fellow British animals know the cull is bad for the environment, but they aren't able to convey this information to human decision-makers.

On the other hand, Boo could. She had a special gift, and it came with a moral duty. She didn't just *want* to help animals; she *had to.* And although she loved the idea of working with Ellie to advance conservation, communicating with animals was her thing. Did she really want Ellie getting involved?

NINE

TWINKLING LIGHTS, ADVENTUROUS NIGHTS

By the time Ellie began packing for the Christmas holidays, Boo had decided: she wanted to meet Eloise on her own, but Boo couldn't imagine relaying this decision to Ellie. Ellie would be offended – and perhaps angry – which caused Boo a great deal of guilt and anxiety.

Just before Ellie zipped up the last of their suitcases, Boo leapt into one.

"Come on, Boo," said Ellie. "We're in a bit of a rush!"

"I just, I have to tell you something," said Boo. She'd finally mustered the courage to tell Ellie that she wanted to meet Eloise by herself and needed to get the words out NOW.

Ellie lifted the top of the suitcase and began to close it, causing Boo to jump out.

"We can talk on the train," responded Ellie curtly. "Now isn't a good time."

Boo had spent the last few days excitedly thinking about Christmas with her grandparents. She couldn't wait to see their house in the countryside, which Ellie called 'cute as a button', and she'd heard so much about her grandma's cooking, she'd become bored by her normal food. Having heard that her grandpa was a legendary gift-giver, Boo had spent hours contemplating what to give him for Christmas. It was all so exciting. As much as Boo loved her life with Ellie, she was ecstatic about being part of a family again – even if it was made up of people.

Ellie should have been over the moon, too – she hadn't been home in months, nor had she introduced Boo to her parents – but she was a giant ball of stress. She'd just handed in a term paper and was already worrying about her next project. Boo encouraged her to relax, to take a break from the demands of school, but Ellie snapped back at her, saying that Boo couldn't possibly understand the pressures of a master's degree.

Even on the train (a place she loved), Ellie looked tired and distracted. She briefly glanced out the window, but her eyes were blank; she spent most of the journey texting her classmates about their upcoming research project.

Boo tried to lighten the mood by being silly and telling jokes, but they fell flat. She twirled around her seat and even chased her tail, which always elicited a chuckle from Ellie, but Ellie's eyes remained fixed on her phone. It was no use. The conservation student was in a nasty mood.

Boo decided to hold off on discussing her desire to meet Eloise alone. Besides, Ellie hadn't brought it up in days. They'd confirmed a time and place with Eloise several days ago, but Ellie hadn't mentioned the meeting since.

The train came to a stop at Charlbury station, where patches of grass glistened beneath a light winter frost. Ellie lugged her suitcases with one arm and balanced Boo's carrier with the other, nearly tripping over a curb, when all of a sudden two white-haired people bundled in puffy coats bounded towards her.

"Ellie, darling!" squealed her mum. "Is it really you?"

Boo pressed her face against the mesh sides of the carrier so she could watch as Ellie hugged her parents. Ellie started smiling – finally.

Ellie's father hugged his daughter so tightly, he practically flattened Boo. She let out a little meow to remind the happy human family of her presence.

"Oh, dear," he said. "I hope Boo's alright."

His big brown eyes appeared at the carrier door. "How do you do, miss Boo?" he asked while pressing his nose against the mesh for what he called an Eskimo kiss. Boo said she was great and asked how he was in return, but he turned away. Over the preceding weeks, Boo confirmed that no people (besides Ellie) understood her when she spoke, but she and Ellie had both hoped that Ellie's parents would be able to verbally communicate with their feline granddaughter.

"We share the same DNA!" Ellie proclaimed one evening. "If I can hear you, I'm sure they can, too."

It quickly became clear that Ellie's optimism was misplaced, for Boo spent the entire car ride trying to engage Mr and Mrs Caldwell in conversation, but they never responded to a thing she said, and at one point Mr Caldwell remarked on Boo's meowing as if it were an annoyance.

Despite this, Boo liked her grandparents immediately. They were warm and chatty and, best of all, they let Boo out of the carrier as soon as everyone piled into the car.

"Let me get a look at you," said Mrs Caldwell. "Dare I say, your and Ellie's eyes are the exact same shade of green! You take after your mum," she said with a chuckle.

Back at the house, Mr Caldwell took Ellie and Boo's things upstairs while Mrs Caldwell put on the kettle.

Pouring a dollop of milk into a small saucer, she asked Ellie if Boo might like a treat.

"Of course," responded Ellie. "Thanks, Mum."

Boo lapped it up greedily before inspecting the cottage. Although the Caldwells no longer lived on the farm where Ellie grew up, their cottage was far bigger than Ellie's student flat, and it was full of quirky nooks and crannies. There were shelves everywhere, a soft window seat that looked upon a garden, and under the stairs, Boo discovered a small storage space where the Caldwells kept their boots. It smelt peculiar and was full of spiderwebs, but Boo knew it would make the BEST hiding place during a game of hide-and-seek.

Ellie sat between her parents on their plush blue sofa sipping tea, colour finally returning to her face. She smiled and laughed as she told them about her life in Cambridge, her green eyes shining like the Christmas tree's twinkling lights dancing across the ceiling. When she asked whether they planned to get another pet, having lost their beloved dog nearly a year ago, they said that they were holding off in case Ellie and Boo decided to spend the summer in Oxfordshire. "This is Boo's home, too," said Mr Caldwell with smiling eyes.

Boo wanted to join the Caldwells for a cuddle but knew she should leave them alone for a family catch-up. Besides, she was eager to check Ellie's Instagram to see if Eloise had responded to her most recent message. In it, Boo asked whether Eloise planned to invite other animals to their meeting.

Boo quietly climbed the cottage's carpeted stairs, sniffing her way to Ellie's room, which was precious but unexpected. The bedroom walls were covered in floral wallpaper, and Ellie's childhood bedspread was light pink. Boo chuckled as she considered how this girly room compared to Ellie's current aesthetic, which was earthy – no pink in sight.

Boo spotted Ellie's phone on the bed and was elated to discover a new message from Eloise.

I look forward to making your acquaintance this Saturday at 6pm. As I said in my previous message, I'll meet you in Wychwood Forest. My husband Fred is joining me, as are several of my neighbours.

Mainly badgers, but we'll have a mix. Look for the hollow oak tree twenty metres from the first fork in the road.

Perfect, thought Boo. There would be multiple badgers, ensuring a range of perspectives, plus several other types of animals, some of whom had been instrumental in relating messages between regions. Birds, in particular, were crucial since they could fly between areas far faster than mammals could walk or run.

Now she just had to tell Ellie that she wanted to take the meeting alone…

Ellie came upstairs for an afternoon nap soon after, and Boo decided it was time to break the news, but as soon as she mentioned the meeting, Ellie interrupted her.

"There's something I want to talk to you about, Boo," she said.

"Me too, actually."

"Me first," Ellie continued. "I really want to meet Eloise, but I have so much work to do. I don't think I can carve out the time. Would that be really disappointing?"

Boo began to smile but held it in.

"That would be fine," said Boo.

They curled up for a catnap, both of them relieved by the other's reaction. *Things are working out just as they should*, thought Boo before drifting off to sleep.

It was already dark when Ellie borrowed her parents' car and drove Boo towards the forest where she'd arranged to meet Eloise and her motley crew of animal activists. Ellie couldn't help but worry about Boo's solitary journey into the forest. She must have asked Boo if she was okay going alone ten times, and she forced Boo to take a small torch with her even though Boo's night vision meant she wouldn't need it.

"Be careful," she warned when dropping Boo off at the edge of the forest. "And don't forget. I'll be at the Plough Inn studying for the next two hours, and then I'll return to this very spot to collect you."

"I get it," said Boo, "and don't worry about me. I'm a farm cat, remember?"

Boo jumped out of the car and began walking towards the forest, turning around once to give Ellie a confident 'I've got this' look.

As she passed between two mighty oak trees, Boo paused to look up and into the forest canopy. She took a deep breath, feeling instantly relaxed, and savoured the complex smells of the forest. Boo walked on, keeping an eye out for the fork Eloise mentioned, when she heard a crash several metres ahead. It startled her, scared her even, but then she heard the familiar sound of laughter echoing throughout the trees.

"Got you!" squealed a sweet young voice. "You can't hide from me!"

Boo focused her gaze and soon spotted two owlets leaping across the forest floor. One of them saw Boo and froze, whispering to the other, "Cat! Cat! We've got to go find Mum."

"It's okay," said Boo, who took two slow steps backwards to demonstrate that she wasn't a threat. Boo added, "I'm a friend, not a foe."

The owlets appeared to relax but huddled together trembling. Their feathers were just starting to appear in funny-looking patches. *They look like cotton balls with eyes and beaks*, thought Boo.

Boo made their acquaintance and asked if they knew Eloise. They did. One pointed its grey wing towards a clearing. "You'll find her over there," she said.

Based on her correspondence, Boo expected Eloise to be formal and intimidating, but Boo was pleasantly surprised to discover that she was just as warm as Boris and Bonnie. She greeted Boo with a big hug and two kisses (one on either cheek) before introducing Boo to her friends.

There were many more animals gathered in the forest than Boo had anticipated. She figured Eloise might bring four or five friends, but there were upwards of forty animals milling around.

Eloise whistled. "Listen up, everyone," she said. "Our special visitor, Boo, has arrived, and she only has an hour or so to spend with us, so let's get down to business."

Eloise produced a small wooden gavel from her pocket and pounded it on a tree stump.

"I hereby call this meeting to order," she proclaimed. (Perhaps Eloise was formal after all!) "I'd like to commence our meeting by allowing Boo to say a few words."

Boo wasn't prepared to give a speech and wondered if she was up for the challenge. Time stood still as she grappled with a sudden pang of self-doubt. She was still a young cat, had only begun learning about conservation several months ago, and she didn't have any real ability to affect change, did she?

Eloise picked up on Boo's anxiety and extended a soft arm towards the kitten. "It's alright," she whispered, "just tell them who you are."

Boo summoned internal strength and began, "Well, hello, everyone. At my core, I'm a simple farm cat, but I was adopted by a human conservation student several months ago."

"What's that?" asked a gruff grey squirrel.

"It's, umm, it means that she's studying to become a protector of animals. She works with other people and organisations to better understand what's happening to animals and wild places across the world so she can ensure we are looked after."

"Typical," said a pheasant standing near Eloise. "People always think they know what's best for us."

"That's where Boo comes in," suggested Eloise loudly over whispers and grumbles.

"My human, Ellie, and I can communicate," said Boo. This statement elicited several laughs, as well as a few oohs and aahs. "It's true," Boo continued, with greater confidence in her voice. "We want to work together, with all of you, to make an impact. We're determined to stop the badger cull."

"Here here!" shouted Eloise.

"But I need to understand what's happening in places like the Cotswolds," stated Boo, "before Ellie and I put together a plan to stop the cull. We need insider information from animals on the ground. That's where YOU come in."

The crowd clapped excitedly. It was clear that Boo had gotten through to the doubters, and several animals were so eager to share insights and ideas, they called out to Boo and Eloise simultaneously.

"Quiet!" said Eloise, banging her gavel once more. "Let's do this in an orderly fashion."

She proceeded to call on animals one by one, carefully recording their statements in a small notebook. Boo listened intently and was fascinated by everything she heard. As it turned out, all species were concerned about the cull. While badgers had the most to lose, other species feared the cull's impact on their health, land, and livelihoods. And as a wise raven observed, "If the British government is comfortable killing badgers, what does that say about the government's respect for British nature and wildlife?"

Most importantly, Boo discovered that badgers living in Oxfordshire and the Cotswolds had spent months recording every mention of forthcoming culls – both in newspapers and among locals – while conducting covert intelligence operations to predict when and where the first phase of the cull might take place. A highly intelligent harvest mouse even built a recording device, from scratch, that she placed under the bar of the pub where local farmers liked to assemble. Local animals knew which politicians favoured culls and which farmers planned to participate, and they were in the process of crafting an escape plan for badgers in case the cull went forward. This information was invaluable; it was precisely what Boo and Ellie needed to develop a strategic media campaign to shift the tide of public opinion. Although Eloise and her friends lacked media savvy, most of them used email and social media on a regular basis and promised to keep in touch with Boo over the coming weeks.

Boo checked the time; like Cinderella at midnight, she had to go.

As she said goodbye to Eloise and her friends, it began to snow. Until now, Boo had only ever seen snow on television. Ellie tried explaining it to her once but failed to find the right words. It was icy, she'd started to say, or was it soft?

Boo spun around, leapt in the air, and stuck her tongue out. She wanted to taste, touch, and smell the snow. It was unlike anything she'd ever experienced before, and that was the point. Nature, she considered, is full of magic… and surprises.

"Four days until Christmas."

"Three days and sixteen hours until Christmas."

"Three days and fourteen hours until Christmas."

"Three days and 1.5 hours until Christmas."

"Boo," said Ellie, "you can't keep counting down this way. I know that you're excited about your first Christmas, but you're driving me crazy."

Boo was on Ellie's bedroom floor clumsily wrapping gifts for Mr and Mrs C, as she now called them, while Ellie sat at her childhood desk flipping through textbooks and furiously typing on her laptop.

"Fine," responded Boo, "but you're no fun. You're supposed to be on a break, remember?"

Ellie swivelled her chair around. "Tell me about it," she said. "This research is suffocating me."

"Why don't we do something spontaneous, like go on a hike? Or play in the snow? You promised we'd do snow angels!"

"I know, I know. I'm sorry. The problem is, one of my classmates offered to review the outline of my lion essay, but she can't get it back to me before the New Year unless I send it to her today."

Boo's smile faded as she set her half-wrapped gifts aside. She needed some time alone. Ellie was already back to her studies and didn't even notice when Boo left the bedroom seconds later.

This 'vacation' wasn't anything like what Boo had imagined. She assumed Ellie would relax once she got to her parents' house, and Boo had pictured the two of them playing games, cooking, and singing Christmas carols with the Caldwells, but instead Ellie spent all of her time in her room reading. Every morning, Boo sat with the Caldwells after breakfast. They loved chatting about Christmas and reliving happy memories. One morning, they played a game where each of them had to guess the other's favourite Christmas memory. Unfortunately, Mr C's answer, which involved the couple's first Christmas with Ellie, caused Mrs C to cry.

"She's never home," said Mrs C glumly, "and even when she is, she ignores us."

Boo jumped onto her grandmother's lap, hoping her presence would comfort her, but it was no use: the Caldwells were just as frustrated as Boo.

Ellie must have realised that Boo was upset because she came looking for the kitten soon after Boo tucked into a cosy nook in the attic.

"Something told me you'd be up here hiding out," she said as she lowered herself to the ground.

"I'm not hiding," corrected Boo.

"You know what I mean," said Ellie with a wink.

Boo didn't smile or wink back. She was not amused.

Ellie tried again. "Look, I know that I've been distracted lately, and I'm genuinely sorry about that. But I'm going to make it up to you."

Boo perked up. "Is that right?"

"It is. I'm going to put all of my work aside for the next three days and however many minutes until Christmas."

Boo checked Ellie's wristwatch. "Fifty-five."

The two erupted into a fit of laughter.

"What about your outline?" asked Boo.

"I can get my classmate's feedback after the holidays. After Boxing Day, I'll resume my research, but I'll be sure to carve out free time every day so we can enjoy quality time with Mum and Dad."

As Ellie mentioned her parents, tears gathered in the corners of her eyes. She wiped them away quickly and began to stand up.

At first Boo felt confused by Ellie's sudden display of emotion. She was so lucky to have her parents in her life – and living so close by – but Boo eventually realised that it's hard for ambitious people like Ellie to balance educational and professional pursuits against family and friendships.

To Boo's surprise, Ellie kept her word, and the next few days were magical. Ellie, her parents, and Boo spent hours sitting by the fire chatting, and Mrs C cooked the most delicious food Boo had ever tasted (Ellie seemed to think so, too, for after every meal, she leaned back in her chair grinning from ear to hear with a look of contentment Boo hadn't observed in months). And, just as Ellie foretold, Mr C gave the best Christmas gifts in the WORLD.

He gave Ellie a leather-bound photo album containing her best pictures from Africa, he bought Mrs C a gorgeous necklace engraved with all of the family's birthdates, and he knitted Boo a wool scarf for chilly days (and camping trips). Even when Ellie resumed her research after Boxing Day, the family spent plenty of quality time together. They went on walks around the village, and the Caldwells even snuck Boo into an early evening screening of *Elf* at the local cinema.

The most uneventful moments were delightful, too: Boo loved being in a house that had windows and a back garden and space to unwind on her own. It felt completely different from life at Darwin College – things were warmer here (not in the literal sense, of course) and more relaxed. But Boo knew that she and Ellie had to return to Cambridge, and when the day came, she felt a mix of emotions. She was sad to say farewell to her grandparents and their charming home, but she also knew it was time to get back to her and Ellie's routine. Besides, they had work to do: Ellie had to continue conducting lion research while juggling classes, and Boo needed to advance the anti-cull campaign. Just last night, Eloise sent a worrisome message indicating that the cull could commence as early as mid-February.

Boo tried to talk to Ellie about the campaign once they got home, but Ellie threw a wrench in Boo's plan by rushing off the library for a late-night research session.

TEN

THE SQUIRRELS WHO
KNEW CHURCHILL

S ince Ellie was working, Boo figured she might as well, too,
so she powered up the iPad Ellie gave Boo for Christmas,
which was pre-owned and only to be used for campaigning
purposes. The first few days with it were disastrous: Boo
would extend her claws, thinking they'd help her activate
the screen, but she kept accidentally turning the device off
instead. Having finally mastered its fickle controls, Boo
logged on to the 'Kill the Cull' Facebook group she and
Eloise created after their meeting to find that a mute swan
named Muhammad had just posted an intriguing message:

If we're going to call off the cull, we should host a rally outside the Houses of Parliament. I have event planning experience and live in St James's Park, so I'm perfectly positioned to manage logistics.

Boo hadn't considered a protest before. No one had. Boo and her fellow activists had focused on crafting compelling social media content and creating escape plans if the cull went forward, but this seemed like a much better idea – one that might nip the problem in the bud. Boo suddenly remembered something Eloise mentioned a while ago: a red squirrel she knew had political connections. The ironically named Lord Brown had friends with political influence, for his ancestor befriended Winston Churchill's pet poodle Rufus in the 1950s while living near 10 Downing Street. Through Rufus, he became acquainted with a number of pets belonging to MPs, as well as animals living in and near the Houses of Parliament. The relationships he built trickled down the family line, and some were still active today, as evidenced by Lord Brown's title. They'd also led to identifiable successes. In the early '90s, when John Major was Prime Minister and George HW Bush was the President of the United States, Bush's beloved spaniel, Millie Kerr Bush, became pen pals with Humphrey the cat, the 'Chief Mouser' then living at 10 Downing Street. Rumour has it, their friendship bolstered Major and Bush's Gulf War efforts.

If Eloise and Boo could get in touch with Lord Brown, they might be able to influence politicians; at the very least, they could get a hold of crucial confidential information, such as whether certain MPs planned to support legislation involving forthcoming badger culls. And thanks to Muhammad's event planning skills, the group could simultaneously organise a protest.

Boo rapidly typed up a new post proposing this joint call to arms. She sought suggestions for next steps and reiterated that she could secure information about how culls negatively impact the environment from Ellie. Boo also hoped that Ellie and her Cambridge conservation network would participate in the rally, but she couldn't make any promises. Privately, she wondered if Ellie would set aside *any* time to join the fight.

Responses started flooding in, and many contained good ideas. Boo couldn't help but giggle when reading some of the more creative ones: an artistically inclined grasshopper offered to design flyers for the protest; and a blue tit named Bruno said he'd write a song – an anthem of sorts – that animals could learn in advance of public events. A pipistrelle bat promised to put together a target list of MPs by party affiliation and district. Eloise, meanwhile, suggested that animals living in the same regions plan in-person meetings over the coming weeks to maximise the power of brainstorming sessions and ensure that momentum carried forward.

As she looked through Ellie's window to the gardens below, Boo decided to host a meeting at Darwin College during the first week of February. It would have to be late at night. Otherwise, she and her animal colleagues risked bumping into students who would undoubtedly wonder why dozens of different species were congregating at Darwin. She created a new Facebook event proposing midnight on Wednesday 5th February.

Ellie still hadn't returned to the flat when Boo's eyelids began to droop with exhaustion, so she put herself to bed. Lying in a cosy ball at the foot of Ellie's bed, Boo entered a half-awake, half-asleep state in which she pictured a diverse group of animals greeting and conversing with one another. They were sitting by a river, weeping willow trees all around them, excitedly discussing the badger cull protest. Fuelled by enthusiasm and optimism, Boo led a group discussion that occasionally erupted into loud bursts of clapping. Then, all of a sudden, a wave of distress washed over her.

She stopped speaking and looked all around before calling out, "Ellie! Where's Ellie?!?"

Boo's nose twitched as she drifted into a deep sleep.

When Boo awoke the next morning, she remembered having a bad dream but couldn't recall what it was about. She closed her eyes and concentrated, hoping she could bring it into focus, but it didn't work. She stretched, leapt off the bed, and trotted to the living room where Ellie was sitting on the sofa pensively sipping tea. Boo jumped onto the couch and into Ellie's lap.

"Good morning, little one," said Ellie. "Are you alright? You were twitching and yowling all night. I tried to wake you at one point, but you were sleeping like a log."

"I had a nightmare," responded Boo. "Annoyingly, I don't know what it was about. Don't you hate when that happens?"

Ellie nodded and then scooted Boo to the side so she could stand up. In the kitchen, she hurriedly rinsed her mug before tossing her laptop into her backpack.

"In a hurry?" asked Boo in a slightly passive-aggressive tone.

"As always," said Ellie. "Today's a big day. We're presenting our initial research, remember?"

Yes, Boo remembered.

"It's a big day for me, too," added Boo. "I have a blog post to write."

Ellie grabbed her keys and opened the front door. "Oh, right," she said. "Best of luck, Boo!"

Just like that, she was gone.

Boo didn't dwell on her hurt feelings, for she didn't have time. She had emails to write and a blog post to draft. She'd never written an article, speech, or blog post before, and she had dozens of emails to sift through.

In her inbox was a message containing an email address for Martha Brown – niece of Lord Brown – who evidently travelled to Cambridgeshire every few months en route to London from her home in the Peak District. *That's convenient*, thought Boo. *Maybe the two could meet for tea in Cambridge?*

Boo eagerly composed a message to Martha proposing the idea, careful to use the formal language she'd picked up from Eloise. *Dear Madam*, it began, and *Sincerely Yours*, it ended.

Her blog post was next. Eloise had suggested that Boo publish a post introducing a wide variety of readers to the cull, but Boo felt incredibly intimidated by the task. She wasn't a writer or conservationist; Boo didn't have any degrees or professional experience. She was just a humble farm cat who cared about animals and the environment; could she really inform and inspire others?

It suddenly began to rain, which exacerbated Boo's blue mood. She ran into the bedroom, tears welling in her eyes, and crawled under the duvet. In that moment, Boo experienced what Ellie later called 'impostor syndrome'. Boo lost sight of her strengths and successes and believed herself unworthy of her role as a conservation advocate. *It's all too much*, thought Boo.

After a short catnap, Boo felt better. She was able to quiet her fears of inadequacy and return to work. She even had an idea for a blog post title, which was, if nothing else, a start.

OUR BADGERS, OUR BROTHERS

BY BABOON CALDWELL

All across the country, Boo typed, *badgers are in danger. The black-and-white animals may be British icons, but politicians want to see them… dead…*

No, thought Boo, *the word 'dead' is too harsh – too real.* She backed up the cursor, instead writing 'gone'.

Before Boo realised it, she had written four hundred words about badgers and the cull, and when she read the post aloud, she felt a surge of pride. *Maybe I am a writer after all*, thought Boo as she lingered on her closing sentence, which read, *Join British badgers and your fellow countrymen, women, and animals in the fight of your life. And remember: governments that care don't cull.*

A new hashtag was born: *#caredontcull.*

The day before the midnight meeting, Boo felt anxious yet excited. She had a morning tea scheduled with Martha Brown, after which she'd bake snacks to bring to her wild animal network. Ellie had recently shown her how to make flapjacks that were packed with dried fruit, nuts, and seeds, and could therefore be eaten by a range of animals.

It was a spectacular day in Cambridge, one of the sunniest Boo had ever seen. She spent a half hour slowly wandering through Darwin's beautiful gardens before crossing the bridge on Silver Street. From there, she looked down on the wooden punting boats for which Cambridge is known. At this hour, punting guides were just beginning to lay down fresh blankets on their vessels with hopes of attracting tourists. Boo walked down the steps towards The Anchor pub and bumped into a friendly guide she'd met on a walk with Ellie one evening (he loved cats, he'd told Ellie). He stroked Boo's silky fur before picking her up for a proper cuddle. Boo licked his face and pressed her body against his warm fleece. Peering over his shoulder, she saw a young red squirrel sitting on a blue-and-white gingham blanket. It must be Martha. Boo jumped down and walked over to say hello.

"I'm Martha Brown," said the beautiful squirrel. She extended her right paw to Boo as if to shake it the way humans do. Boo gave her a half-shake, half-fist bump that made both of them giggle.

Martha had a leather-bound notebook and a small hamper containing tea and treats, which she invited Boo to sample as soon as the kitten sat down on the comfy chequered blanket.

As they sipped tea from delicate porcelain glasses, Martha opened the diary and explained its contents.

"My ancestor kept meticulous notes," she said. "He recorded every meeting he had with the pets of high-ranking members of government, like Churchill's dog, and kept contact information and family trees whenever it was available."

Boo admired the beautiful cursive writing adorning each page. It was loopy and symmetrical and so very old-fashioned.

"It's been passed down through the generations and updated as well, so we have current information about many Members of Parliament and contacts for their animal companions."

"That's amazing!" squealed Boo. "So, we can just text their dogs and email their cats?"

"It's best if my uncle does so on our behalf," said Martha with a wink, "for he's the one with personal relationships. The good news," she continued, "is that he supports the plan you've hatched. For the protest, I mean."

"I have a question," said Boo with a puzzled look on her face. "How do high-profile pets influence the politics of their humans?"

"Great question, Boo. The truth is, it's more of an art than a science. Many animals say that when they focus on particular ideas and information, their owners seem to pick it up somehow."

Boo nodded with familiarity.

"Others lay out information sheets and reports that my uncle helps craft for their political owners to see. This seems to work very nicely," finished Martha.

"That's wonderful!" Boo clasped her front paws together, accidentally knocking her teacup over. "My goodness, I'm clumsy," said Boo meekly. But Martha didn't seem to mind. She turned Boo's cup upright and filled it with fresh tea.

Boo proceeded to tell Martha about the meeting she'd planned for the following evening and asked if she could attend.

Martha couldn't attend, unfortunately, for she was off to London to see her uncle that very afternoon, but she'd email Boo an update that could be shared at the meeting.

Things are coming together beautifully, thought Boo as she enjoyed a final sip of tea, but one worry remained.

Weeks ago, Ellie promised to put together a short report on how the cull would negatively impact the environment beyond damaging badgers, but despite multiple reminders from Boo, Ellie had yet to produce anything. Boo appreciated that Ellie's schoolwork came first, and she knew that Ellie often drilled into a task to the exclusion of others, but Lord Brown would need Ellie's report when speaking to his contacts. As Martha explained, politicians are exceptionally busy; getting their attention isn't easy. Making a case for halting the call would require information about how culls impact people and economic interests.

"Damage to wild animals," said Martha, "is rarely enough."

Back at the flat, Boo wrote down a draft speech for the next day's meeting before getting her paws dirty baking in the kitchen. When Ellie returned a few hours later, Boo had flour all over her face.

"You look like a ghost!" proclaimed Ellie. "A ghost cat!"

She seemed to be in exceptional spirits and was home much earlier than usual. *She must have skipped the library*, thought Boo.

Ellie unzipped her backpack and handed a batch of papers to Boo.

"I know it took me a while," she said, "but I finally finished the report I promised you."

Boo grinned. "Thank you!" she exclaimed.

Boo read it over and was pleased to see that it utilised simple language; the short report contained plenty of information but was written in a way that anyone could understand.

Boo leapt into Ellie's arms, practically knocking the student over, and licked her face for a solid minute.

"You're welcome, Boo," said Ellie. "Now tell me about this meeting."

ELEVEN

MIDNIGHT BY THE RIVER CAM

Boo nearly tripped over a fallen tree branch as she carried a heavy plate of flapjacks towards the riverbank.

She and Ellie had stayed up late the night before going over Ellie's report and Boo's draft speech. This meeting, they agreed, was critical. It was one thing for animals across the UK to come together online but quite another to bring them together for a large-scale political protest. And although Muhammad had done an incredible job connecting with other event-savvy Londoners to work on protest logistics, Ellie had drawn Boo's attention to the fact that regional organisers like Boo would need to arrange transport for the day of the event. How would dozens of animals living in and around Cambridge get to London? Boo wasn't sure. She'd need to put her thinking cap on for this one.

Before they fell asleep, Ellie promised to attend the midnight meeting, but she'd have to meet Boo and the others there since she had an evening study session with classmates that could run late.

Boo checked the time on her iPad: 11:30pm. No sign of Ellie.

She took a deep breath and told herself that Ellie would arrive any minute. She had promised.

Boo sat by the bank of the River Cam peering into its glossy swirls. She watched small insects glide across the surface and kept her eyes peeled for birds or otters swimming her way. A few mallard ducks arrived, followed by swans and coots. Boo said hello to her new friends and then responded to a loud greeting coming from a squirrel hugging a nearby oak tree. Darwin College was buzzing with animal activity. But where was Ellie?

At 11:55, Boo zipped around the garden sharing flapjacks. *If nothing else, these animals won't go home hungry*, she thought. She was nervous – this was the first time she'd led a meeting by herself – and frustrated by the fact that Ellie hadn't arrived as promised. But Boo couldn't afford to melt down. The show had to go on. She thought about Eloise and the encouragement she'd given Boo during their gathering in the forest. Boo could do this.

Standing beneath a bright half-moon, Boo began to speak.

"Good evening, everyone," she said a little nervously. "Thank you so much for coming. As you know by now, the government is planning a large-scale badger cull that threatens thousands of badgers across the UK." Boo looked around to see if any badgers had appeared. "Unfortunately," she continued, "we don't seem to have any badgers with us this evening."

A tiny voice piped up from the garden's edge. "I'm here," it squeaked. "My family couldn't make it, but I'm here to represent them."

"Excellent," said Boo. "And welcome."

Boo started by briefing the group on her contacts in the Cotswolds who continued to work undercover to identify when and where the cull's first phase would take place.

"We have reason to believe that the cull could commence on 11th March, which is just over four weeks away."

"My God!" yelled a wood pigeon. "That soon?"

"It seems so," responded Boo stoically. "Which leaves us little time to prepare."

"Are we gonna rally or what?" shouted a hedgehog sitting beside a nearby shrub. "We've gotta do something!"

Animals began chattering away. Their strained facial expressions made their anxiety clear.

"We are!" Boo shouted over the murmuring crowd. She felt a wave of strength come over her. "We'll storm Parliament if we have to!"

The shy badger who spoke previously stood up and ran towards Boo. "Thank you!" she shouted as she approached her feline friend. She hugged Boo tightly and turned to face the others. "Thank all of you!"

As soon as things quieted down, Boo asked animals to raise their hands if they were interested in attending the protest in London. To Boo's surprise and delight, nearly all of them demonstrated interest, but several expressed concerns about logistics. Had a particular day been chosen? How would everyone get to London from Cambridgeshire?

Several dates were under consideration, Boo said, but transport had not been arranged. Did anyone have suggestions?

"Don't s'pose we can all hop on the train?" asked a duck.

"What about a bus?" added a gorgeous mute swan.

"I don't think public transport is an option," answered Boo.

"A charter bus," clarified the swan, who introduced herself as Gemma Garrett. "Perhaps one of the lovely old double-deckers?"

"Now that's an idea," responded Boo. She could visualise it: a motley crew of animals crammed into an English icon with hopes of changing the country for the better.

Just then, a bat hanging upside down from a tree branch spread its wings to ask a question.

"I hate to be a Debbie Downer," she said, "but don't we need people's help to pull this off? None of us is big enough to drive a bus, and, besides, we'll likely run into trouble once we get to London. Sure, some people like us, but others don't. We'd be putting ourselves in danger…"

Boo's stomach churned. "You're right," she acknowledged. "We need people to see this through. And they need us."

Boo cleared her throat and resumed speaking: "As many of you know, my mum, Ellie, is a conservation student who's provided incredible input on our strategy. She was supposed to be here tonight…" Boo trailed off and looked at the ground.

She felt tears welling up in her eyes but quickly brushed them off with her snow-white paws.

"I don't know where she is," she continued shakily. "But she's let me down several times, and I think it's time to consider doing the protest without her."

"We don't need humans!" yelled a field mouse with an impressively loud voice.

"Animals only!" shouted a grey squirrel.

Within seconds, the group began chanting, "Animals only!" at such a high volume, Boo worried that her friends would wake up students residing at Darwin College.

Boo was torn. She loved their energy but knew that without Ellie and her network, the animals would likely fail.

Before she had a chance to speak, Gemma the swan began honking repeatedly until everyone fell silent.

"That is quite enough," she said. "As exciting as 'Animals Only' sounds, we all know that we can't achieve results without the help of people."

Gemma has such stage presence, thought Boo. She was graceful, calm, and commanded attention.

"It's getting late," Gemma continued, "so I suggest we come back down to reality and make plans that will *actually* succeed." She raised one of her wings and pointed it towards Boo. "Boo, you must get Ellie's attention. We need her support – and her network."

Boo nodded, feeling immensely grateful to Gemma for bringing the meeting to order.

"I will arrange transport," said Gemma. "And the rest of you must carry on spreading the word to friends and family. Those who can't attend the rally in London can still help by generating support online."

"That's right," said Boo after checking the time and seeing that it was nearly 1:00am. "I encourage all of you to regularly visit our Facebook and Instagram pages, and please continue using hashtags like #killthecull, #caredontcull, and #badgerlove on all of your social media channels."

"We're in the home stretch," Boo mumbled to herself as she made her way back to the flat. "We're nearly there."

TWELVE

HIDDEN TUNNELS

When Boo stumbled into the flat at 1:15am, she encountered Ellie fast asleep on the sofa – in her clothes, sitting upright, near a mug of now-cold tea. Boo couldn't help but smile when she realised what had happened: Ellie had rushed back for the meeting but was so tired, she needed a cuppa to stay awake. Unfortunately, Ellie made the mistake of sitting down to drink it, accidentally falling asleep before taking a single sip.

Boo realised in that moment that Ellie was trying her best. Ellie wanted to be present and helpful, but the master's course was running her ragged, at times depleting all of her energy.

Boo trotted to the bedroom and returned dragging a small blanket that she delicately placed over Ellie like a mother would a child. This act – of looking after Ellie the way Ellie had looked after Boo – warmed the tabby's heart. She was soon asleep herself, curled up beside Ellie, and the night passed without a single nightmare.

In the morning, Ellie apologised profusely, and Boo happily accepted the apology as the two sat down for breakfast. Toast and orange juice for Ellie; cat's milk and fish-flavoured treats for Boo. Ellie wanted to hear all about the meeting. Boo got nervous during the 'Animals Only' part (Ellie could tell because Boo's eyes got really wide, and she forgot to blink), and they were both relieved when Boo came to the story's ending.

"You do need people," said Ellie. "And we need you!"

The coming days were the busiest of Boo's life. She was online constantly – trading messages with protest planners, responding to questions on social media, and conducting research into positive environmental impacts produced by badgers. Boo was so busy, in fact, she didn't notice when Ellie began leaving earlier in the morning and returning later at night. It finally dawned on Boo that she and Ellie were like two ships passing in the night: they were sharing the same flat but barely saw each other.

Boo had a giant paper calendar spread out on the coffee table that helped her keep track of the many things that needed to be accomplished before the protest, which now had a fixed date and time: Wednesday 4th March 2020 at 2:00pm, an hour before Parliament was due to debate the merits of badger culls. As fate would have it, Ellie's lion paper was due on the morning of Friday 6th March – but the protest couldn't wait. Intelligence coming in from the Cotswolds showed the first round of the cull taking place on the 16th, which gave the protesters just enough time to halt the cull before it began. It was going to be tough, but Boo, Eloise, Martha, and their legion of animal activists were guardedly optimistic. They might just pull this off.

The morning of 28th February was grey and drizzly, the kind of morning that makes you want to stay in bed all day, but Boo had to get up and start ticking items off of her to-do list. She had breakfast and powered up her iPad, opening her inbox to incredible news: Lord Brown's lobbying efforts had compelled two senior members of Parliament, one from the Labour Party, another a Tory, to publicly condemn the cull. Not only that, they intended to introduce legislation banning all future badger culls during the debate scheduled for the afternoon of 5th March.

Boo was dizzy with happiness – literally. The living room was spinning like a tornado zipping through a Texas town when Boo placed her iPad on the table, laid her head down, and began taking several deep breaths.

When Boo's balance returned, she sat up and shouted, "Woohooo!" at the top of her lungs. Boo didn't care if everyone at Darwin College heard her raucous meowing! She and her friends had made astonishing progress – and in an incredibly short period of time. Boo wasn't the type to congratulate herself, but she felt a surge of pride so massive, she literally patted herself on the back. All of her efforts were paying off, and everything in her life felt aligned. She was happy, successful, and optimistic. Maybe a simple farm cat could change the world after all?

Boo immediately shared the good news on Facebook and Instagram and then called Martha to get further details.

Boo was relieved to discover that Martha and Lord Brown had assembled a team of animals based in London who could report back on, and influence, MPs, for as much as Boo wanted to visit the capital, she didn't have time to zip down before the protest. There was way too much happening in Cambridge and online, and Boo was due to meet a large group of animals the following afternoon to rehearse Bruno the blue tit's anthem.

Bruno had spent many long hours developing lyrics, and the wee bird even choreographed a dance to accompany the song, which was simple-but-elegant and enjoyed a chorus participants could easily remember. ("They're black and white, and out of sight, but Britain's badgers deserve what's right.")

Bruno posted a video on Facebook showing him and his avian friends swaying to the lyrics before breaking apart, shuffling around, and coming back together in the shape of a heart. Boo was blown away by the concept but a little worried about the feasibility of a large group of animals singing and dancing in sync. Practice would make perfect, or so she hoped.

There was also the matter of the double-decker bus. As promised, Gemma took on the task of finding a company that rented out the iconic buses, but unless swans magically developed the ability to drive (and get driving licences), Ellie would have to make the booking *and* drive the group to and from London. After much nudging from Boo, she called to reserve a bus, and she swore up and down that she'd have enough time on 4th March to collect the bus, drive everyone to London, and bring them back that evening. She'd do so by finishing her lion paper several days early, but Boo had her doubts. She'd never seen Ellie finish an assignment early, and this one was incredibly important (Ellie seemed to think that her entire career hinged on its success). Besides, Ellie had broken promises before.

Shockingly, Ellie seemed to be on track. By bedtime on Sunday 1st March, Ellie had completed an initial draft. Editing would take a few days, said Ellie, but she wouldn't have any problem wrapping things up in time for the protest, and, worst-case scenario, she could resume editing on the 5th. She'd stay up all night if she had to.

Monday the 2nd was a beautiful day: sunny and a bit warm – the first hint of spring. Ellie was so relaxed, she slept until 9am (a record, by Boo's tally), and that afternoon, she made Boo put protest planning aside so the two could kayak to Grantchester. Boo thought Ellie was crazy; they both had way too much on their plates, but Ellie said the outing would do them some good. They could use the fresh air.

As Ellie dipped her paddle into the silky green water, she took a deep breath and loudly exhaled. "It's magical out here, isn't it, Boo?"

"It sure is," responded Boo. "Thanks for getting me out of the flat."

"You've been working your bum off!" said Ellie.

Boo responded, "I learnt from the best."

Ellie stopped paddling and turned around to face Boo. "Oh, dear, I hope I haven't made you a workaholic like me!" said Ellie.

"No, not at all," responded Boo with a laugh. "But I did learn about activism from you."

"I'm amazed by you," said Ellie, a single tear rolling down her cheek.

"Are you sad?" asked Boo.

"No, I'm happy," answered Ellie. "These are happy tears. I'm just so… proud of you."

"Of us," corrected Boo. "Proud of us."

Ellie resumed paddling while Boo soaked up the scene. There were graceful swans on the river ahead and robins singing in nearby trees. A dog barked in the distance, sending several mallard ducks crashing into the river, and beside the kayak a fish sent bubbles to the water's surface.

All of a sudden, someone shouted from ahead, "Hey there!"

Boo squinted to see if she could make out the shadowy figure standing on the river's edge.

"Are you Boo?" it asked.

Boo soon realised that she was looking at a red fox – one she'd never met before. It was tiny, about Boo's size when Ellie had adopted her from the shelter, and must have been a kit.

Boo responded, "I am. Have we met?"

"OMG," said the kit as it walked to the edge of the bank. "I've seen you on Instagram. And Facebook! And my parents talk about you ALL the time."

Ellie started giggling and whispered to Boo, "You're a bona fide celebrity." She paddled towards the shore so Boo could meet her number one fan.

"That's so kind of you to say," said Boo. "Do you know about the badger cull?"

"Do I ever," said the smiling kit. "Mum and Dad are hoping to go to London for the protest, but they're worried about leaving my sisters and me at home."

"Why don't you come along?" suggested Boo.

"They say we're too little," said the fox. "But I'm going to watch everything online. I assume you're going to live-stream the event?"

"We sure are," responded Boo, who couldn't believe the tiny fox knew about live-streaming and social media.

The kit wanted to give Boo a high five before saying goodbye, so Boo jumped out of the kayak for a quick fist-bump before rejoining Ellie for the remainder of their journey.

Her celebrity moment was a confidence boost, of course, but more than anything it underscored that Boo and her friends were reaching animals all across the country... and possibly beyond.

Boo and Ellie toasted each other during their picnic, clinking mugs of sparkling lemonade, before sharing their favourite memories. Five months had passed since serendipity brought Boo and Ellie together, but on reflection, it felt as though a lifetime of events had occurred during that short window of time: the duo had bonded and learnt how to communicate, and Boo had discovered that, like Ellie, she was passionate about nature and wildlife. Boo had loved meeting Ellie's parents, and Ellie laughed remembering the times Boo snuck out of their tent on camping trips. Boo countered that the funniest moments occurred when Ellie snuck Boo into her Cambridge classes. "Remember the time I fell asleep and woke myself up snoring?" giggled Boo.

"Want to know the best part?" asked Ellie as they loaded their things into the kayak to return home. "We're just getting started. We have so many adventures ahead!"

When she lay down for bed that night, Boo was so happy, she felt like she might burst. Fears and stresses surrounding the protest momentarily slipped away. All that was left was pure, unadulterated joy.

Unfortunately, something shifted on Tuesday morning. Ellie was gone when Boo got out of bed despite having promised to make the two of them a full English breakfast. A short note on the kitchen counter read, *Change of plan. Off to library. Sorry. Xx*

Boo was too focused on her massive to-do list to worry about Ellie's whereabouts, but as the day went on and her text messages to Ellie went unanswered, she started to wonder if something was wrong.

Is everything okay? 14:51

Please respond. 15:47

Don't forget that we have to pick up the bus tomorrow at 8am. 17:05

Okay, I'm worried. Should I be worried? What's going on? 19:45

At 8pm sharp, Boo joined a group video call with the other key protest planners. Eloise was there. Martha, too. Even Boris logged on to the call. It was clear that everyone was experiencing a range of emotions. They kept talking over one another and nervously giggling, their excitement betraying fear about the protest's success.

Martha shared some very positive news: the two MPs co-proposing legislation banning badger culls had secured its introduction into the forthcoming legislative session. Furthermore, they'd begun raising support for the bill among their peers, and they were confident that it would pass. Fluffy, a ragdoll cat who lived with the Tory proposer, told Lord Brown there were about ten undecided MPs, but she assured him that she had 'an army of animals' nudging their political parents towards supporting the ban.

As Martha explained, the protest could make or break the bill's success. "They want to see a huge turnout," said Martha.

"What does that mean?" asked a rock dove in charge of handing out flyers. "Are we talking hundreds of animal and human participants or thousands?"

The call was eerily silent; no one seemed to know.

Boo read her speech aloud before reminding the group that Ellie would be the one delivering it at the protest to ensure human listeners (and politicians) received the message.

"I wish you could give the speech," said Eloise. "You wrote it, after all."

"I do, too," said Boo. "But Ellie will be great, and this way animals and people will hear our call to arms."

"If she turns up," said a grouchy voice Boo hadn't heard before.

"She will," said Boo defensively. "Now, let's move on."

Bruno reminded everyone about the song and dance routine and insisted on singing the tune several times until everyone on the call had it down.

When the call ended an hour later, Boo checked her email and text messages to see if Ellie had reached out. Nothing. Not a peep.

Boo skipped dinner and anxiously paced across Ellie's bed. In less than twenty-four hours, the protest would be over, and animals across the UK would be miserable or celebratory – at this point, it was anyone's guess – but without Ellie, there was no getting to London, no chance of participating at all.

When Ellie still wasn't home at midnight, Boo's frustration turned to anger. Ellie had mentioned spending all night in the library *after* the protest, not *before*. It was important that she sleep well the night before the big drive to London. Ellie was a confident driver, but she'd never navigated a bus before! Besides, if all she had to do was edit her draft, why was she MIA?

Boo knew a bit about editing and couldn't imagine that it would require more than a day's work. Had something terrible happened? Boo's head spun with worry as she lay down for bed. So many things could have gone wrong: Ellie could have gotten into an accident heading home from the library, or maybe one her parents had fallen ill. In an emergency, Ellie might rush home to see them without first collecting Boo.

Boo considered reaching out to Gemma to discuss alternative arrangements for travelling to London, but she knew from previous conversations in person and online that none of the Cambridge-based animals had human friends like Ellie who could transport the group to London. She also didn't want to alarm the others, especially since they'd need energy and enthusiasm the following day. *Raising alarm bells would do more harm than good*, thought Boo.

Somehow, in the midst of intense anger, anxiety and fear, Boo managed to fall asleep, though the kitten's dreams were tormented. She was in the shelter all alone, lost in the Norfolk Broads, and trapped in a small room without any natural light. Boo had nightmares about the cull and the loss of her badger friends. At one point, she was standing on a podium beside Parliament, singing Bruno's anthem, but she was the only living being in all of London. The city was completely empty. Where had everyone gone?

Boo jolted awake just after 6am, her soft fur coated in sweat. Instinctively, she put her paw on Ellie's side of the bed, finding it empty. She sat up, looked around, jumped off the bed, and inspected the living room and kitchen. It was obvious that Ellie had never come home.

She and Ellie had planned to leave the flat at 7am to collect the bus, and here Boo was, on her own an hour beforehand, with no idea where Ellie was. No new messages were on the iPad, and when Boo called Ellie's phone, it went straight to voicemail. *Must be dead*, thought Boo, and, sure enough, there was the charger – right beside the bed.

Boo began to panic. Her heart rate surged; she felt dizzy. She submerged her head in her water bowl, hoping the cool water would revive her, and lay down on the floor to rest.

When she finally felt restored, she got up and began to brainstorm. *Where could Ellie be? Think, think, think.* "The library," Boo said aloud. "She has to be in the library. She's ALWAYS in the library!"

Boo knew where the university library was located, for Ellie had taken her there several times after sneaking Boo into lectures. Boo was even familiar with Ellie's favourite spot: it was a small desk on the north side of the library, on the fourth floor. Ellie liked it because it was dead quiet and no other students used the space. Ellie would be there.

Boo grabbed her iPad and the spare keys Ellie kept in the kitchen and ran out of the flat at lightning speed, the door slamming behind her. She wasn't supposed to leave the flat without Ellie's permission, but if there was ever a time to break the rules, this was it.

In any event, Ellie couldn't be mad: she was the one who messed up!

Boo raced up Queen's Road, snuck through the fellows' garden at King's College, and reached the entrance to the university library at 6:27am. Using all of her might, and fuelled by adrenaline, she tried to heave the giant metal doors open, but they wouldn't budge. She then attempted to open them by giving herself a running start, but the doors were fixed in place as if glued together. She looked around to see if she was missing something, and that's when she realised that when the library is closed, as it was at this early hour, you could only get inside with a plastic key card. Ellie had one, of course, but Boo was out of luck. She sat on the steps and waited, hoping an eager student or faculty member would appear, but when it approached 7am and no one had come, Boo decided to get creative.

Ellie once told her a story about secret passageways beneath the university. Rumour had it, underground tunnels connected the colleges. *If they existed*, thought Boo, *they'd likely run below the library*. The question was: where to begin looking?

Boo did a quick lap around the library with her eyes peeled for metal grating, staircases, or other features that hinted at a way in. When that didn't work, she sprinted towards a small stream, Bin Brook, located just north of the library. Streams sometimes run underground, so Boo hoped this one might provide a clue.

She hated water – always had – but desperation sent her leaping into the babbling brook without hesitation. Fortunately, the brook wasn't deep, so Boo wasn't forced to swim. Slowly walking along slippery stones, Boo followed the brook towards the library, but the stream veered off to the right before reaching the site of the giant building.

Boo shivered as she scrambled up the bank, and her mood was equally miserable. *This is it*, she thought. She'd tried everything, but there was no way into the library, no way to find Ellie, no way to get to London. The protest would conceivably carry on in Boo's absence, but she was the glue that held everything – and everyone – together.

Tears gathered in Boo's eyes, and she didn't even try to wipe them away. For the first time since the animal shelter, Boo had a good, long cry.

A few minutes later, a voice emerged from behind Boo. "Excuse me," it said. "Are you alright? I hate to disturb you, but I'm a wee bit worried."

Boo turned around and found herself face to face with a female badger wearing a red-and-gold Cambridge scarf.

"I've been better," Boo said with a muffled cry.

The badger walked over to Boo, removed her scarf, and draped it over Boo like a blanket. "There, there," she said. "Can I help?"

"Not unless you know a way into the library," said Boo with a half-hearted laugh.

"Well, well, well," responded the badger. "It's your lucky day."

Boo looked up at the friendly face with wide eyes.

"I'm Gertrude, by the way. Live just over there." She motioned towards a plot of green grass on the edge of the library's north side. "Have for years."

Boo interjected, speaking rapidly. "I'm Boo, it's nice to meet you. I have to get into the library... ASAP... it's an emergency. My mum – well, she's kind of my mum – she's in there, and she's got to drive me to London."

"Slow down, Boo," said Gertrude gently. "Let's get you a cup of tea. Follow me." She stood up and meandered towards her den.

Boo trailed behind. "That sounds nice, but I haven't got the time! Can you get me into the library?"

"Yes, dear, I can. Our den connects to the tunnels all the students go on about. They are real, you see." Gertrude winked.

Boo grabbed Gertrude's hand and nudged her forwards at a faster pace. "Have you heard about the protest happening in London this afternoon?" asked Boo excitedly.

"Of course," said Gertrude. "My family is coming over later to watch it online. We've been signing petitions, sending letters to friends across the country, and we're a part of a Facebook group called 'Kill the Cull'. Have you heard of it, Boo?"

"I started it!" Boo said, practically shouting. "And I'm the one kicking off the protest, but if I don't get inside the library straight away, things will fall apart."

"Oh, goodness me," said Gertrude, now moving faster. "Let's get you inside."

Having finally realised the urgency of the situation, Gertrude picked up the pace. She quickly led Boo through her den, right past the teakettle, and took her to a small wooden door barely visible in dim candlelight. She grabbed a brass key from a concealed shelf, unlocked the door, and said, "Come along, Boo, it's not far."

They walked in silence, Gertrude leading the way, until they reached another door – this one much larger than the first.

"It's a good thing you found me, Boo," said Gertrude as she stepped on her tippy toes and pressed a second key into the door's lock. "Very few people or animals have keys to this door. We got one from the former librarian years ago. He was a kind man who had a special interest in badgers. You'll have to come back for supper sometime so I can tell you the story of how we came to communicate with him."

Boo was too eager to get inside to recognise the significance of what Gertrude just said – that she and her family were able to *communicate* with a human. It wasn't just Boo and Ellie, then. There were others…

Boo gave Gertrude a hug, thanked her profusely for her help, and skittered up the first stairwell she could find. She raced to the fourth floor, spotting a clock on her way. It was 8:14am.

Boo ran through the stacks, their musty smell causing her to sneeze, until she neared Ellie's preferred study spot. "Ellie!" Boo shouted. "Ellie! Are you here?"

Ellie's eyes flicked open. She was asleep in her chair, her face resting on a messy pile of paper.

"What?" she said drowsily as she sat upright. "Where am I?"

"The library!" Boo said with a hint of anger in her voice. "You fell asleep in the library!"

"Oh my God," said Ellie as she scrambled up from her seat. She grabbed her papers, threw them into her bag, and scooped up Boo.

Boo hissed; she couldn't help it. She was upset with Ellie. Furious, even.

"What have I done?" said Ellie as she walked towards the stairs with Boo still in her arms.

"I've let you down. I'm so very sorry." Now Ellie was crying. The morning was turning out to be *quite* emotional.

"It's okay." Boo licked Ellie's tears. "We have time to get the bus and make it to the protest if we leave NOW."

Ellie left her bike at the library and ordered a taxi. She and Boo rode to the bus depot in silence, Ellie stroking Boo's cheeks and chin – Boo's favourite places to be scratched.

As they approached a lot of shiny red buses, she turned to Boo. "Will you ever forgive me?"

"Of course," said Boo.

Driving the bus was harder than Ellie anticipated, but after practising in the parking lot, she hit her stride. "If you can call off a badger cull, I can drive a bus," she joked to Boo.

They had enough time to swing by the flat so Ellie could change clothes and Boo could grab her speech from the table where she'd inadvertently left it several hours earlier. Boo decided to continue wearing Gertrude's scarf, even though it was a bit wet, since the University of Cambridge was part of Boo's conservation journey.

At 10am, they were in the parking lot next to Tennis Court Road. All of Boo's announcements had asked animals to arrive by 10:30 sharp, so Ellie and Boo had a few quiet moments to catch their breath. Boo sat on the top level of the bus making final tweaks to the speech while Ellie popped over to Fitzbillies café for fuel. She returned with dozens of pastries that were a hit with the many animals soon boarding the double-decker.

By 10:45, they were ready to go. Every single seat was taken, and quite a few animals had little ones on their laps.

"Kill the cull!" shouted a stoat dangling from an arm rail.

"Care, don't cull!" added a fluffy robin.

Ellie honked the horn and shouted, "Let's do this!"

Although the journey was marked with laughter, songs, and unbridled enthusiasm, there were sombre moments, too.

Boo spent much of the ride walking up and down the rows greeting her fellow activists. Many were new friends, though conversations quickly revealed that all of these animals, every last one, knew Boo from her online activity. Like the fox kit on the banks of the River Cam, many of them treated Boo like a celebrity; she was a source of activism and inspiration, and animals young and old wanted to hear her story.

At one point, Boo came upon a family of badgers sitting solemnly at the back of the bus. Nervousness was visible in their eyes.

"Will this work?" asked the family patriarch. "Or are we just fooling ourselves?"

Boo was caught off guard. She was so wrapped up in the excitement of the day, she nearly forgot that if the protest failed, thousands of animals could die. Here were eight of them – a beautiful, multi-generational family, putting its hopes in Boo's paws.

Boo took a deep breath and knelt down beside them. "I certainly hope so," she said, "but we will get through this no matter what happens today. Together," she added. "We're in this *together*. This protest and everything that came before it has demonstrated just how connected we are. And it's not just animals. People like Ellie care, too."

A tiny badger cub squirmed out of its mother's embrace and walked over to Boo. Without speaking, it leaned in and gave Boo a giant hug. Neither Boo nor the infant wanted to let go. The moment warmed Boo's heart and lingered in her memory for years to come, for it reminded her why she was fighting so hard against the badger cull and signified the strong bonds Boo had built with animals across the United Kingdom.

"Thank you," the cub's mother whispered when the little one finally let go. She then dug into her purse, producing a small Cambridge University baseball cap, which she handed to Boo.

"To go with your scarf," she said with a smile.

Animals and people surrounded the west side of the Houses of Parliament when Ellie dropped off her animal friends. Boo glanced around, feeling nervous and excited, as she took in the scene: hundreds, maybe thousands, of animals and people of every shape, size, and species stood side by side on Parliament's packed grounds. Many were wearing black and white in honour of badgers, and some sported armbands, hats, and shirts bearing the words 'Kill the Cull'. *That's a surprise*, thought Boo. She had no idea anyone in the anti-cull camp had created gear! She made a mental note to thank the creature behind the cool kit, but she had more important things to do.

Boo used her iPad to call Martha and Eloise to see where they were before pushing through crowds, the Cambridge lot trailing behind her, as she sought out the stage.

"There!" shouted a mallard duck from behind her. "To your left, Boo!"

As Boo rushed towards the stage, she failed to notice that all eyes were on her. Protest participants of various species recognised the heroic tabby. After all, her photo had been splashed across their social media pages for months.

"It's Boo!" called out a young boy. Numerous animals and people in his vicinity began chanting, "Thank you, Boo! Thank you Boo!" over and over again.

Boo didn't hear their chants until she finished scrambling onto the stage. She faced the crowd smiling from ear to ear, her whiskers blowing in the breeze. "Thank YOU!" she called out, momentarily forgetting that human protesters wouldn't hear her words of gratitude. In the chaos, Boo had inadvertently dropped Gertrude's scarf, so she pressed her new baseball cap firmly to her striped head to ensure she held on to at least one of the morning's special gifts.

Boo looked around anxiously. Martha and Eloise were huddled at the back of the stage with a megaphone, a 'Care Don't Cull' banner, and several 'Kill the Cull' signs, but Ellie was nowhere to be seen.

What if she hadn't found a place to park the bus? Worse, what if she'd been arrested? Ellie had warned Boo that police sometimes arrest protesters. Naturally, they wouldn't lock up animals, but Ellie's species was at risk.

"It'll be alright," mouthed Martha. "Give her time."

Time! thought Boo. *We're running out of time!*

The protest was scheduled to begin at 2pm – an hour before Members of Parliament were planning to debate, and possibly vote on, badger culls – so time was of the essence. Lord Brown had his finger on the political pulse within Parliament, and at last count, he said that eight critical votes were still undecided. The protest could, therefore, push wishy-washy members over the edge. As Lord Brown often said, "If you make enough noise, they're bound to listen."

Boo fumbled for her iPad to find the time before realising that Big Ben's imposing metal arms displayed the time for all of London to see. 1:58. Two minutes before the protest's official start!

"Booooo!" screeched Ellie from below the stage. "I'm here!"

She leapt onto the stage like an acrobat, her face dripping with sweat as words poured out of her mouth. "I couldn't find parking, and then this officer stopped me, and I said, 'You have to let me go, sir, lives literally depend on it!'"

"Relax," said Boo, rubbing herself against Ellie's trousers. It was her turn to be a calming force amidst chaos.

"He was threatening to arrest me when Professor Baine appeared out of the blue. I had no idea he – or anyone from the course – was coming, but he said he wouldn't miss it for the world, and then he talked to the officer, and then we ran over here, and— Oh my God, I'm so tired, Boo."

Eloise appeared and handed Ellie a reusable metal water bottle.

Ellie greedily downed its contents, wiped the sweat from her brow, and took a deep breath. She looked at Boo intently. "Okay," she said. "Are you ready?"

"I'm ready," said Boo shakily. "Are you?"

"Ready as I'll ever be…"

Boo climbed up Ellie's body and took a seat on her right shoulder. She dug her claws into Ellie's jumper to ensure she didn't go flying off if Ellie decided to rapidly move around during the speech, as she sometimes did when nervous.

Eloise returned with a red-and-white megaphone, which she placed in Ellie's hands.

"Remember," whispered Boo into Ellie's ear. "I'll read the speech to you word for word. You just have to repeat it to the crowd."

"You got it," answered Ellie as she took several steps forward. "This is all you, Boo. I'm just the messenger."

"We love you, Boo!" shouted a Maine Coon cat from beside the stage. Others whistled and clapped as camera flashes went off like fireworks. Many protesters lifted their phones high into the air so they could document the scene for friends and strangers far and wide.

As Ellie raised the megaphone to her mouth, the crowd went silent.

"Good afternoon, human and animal friends," stated Ellie. "We are here today to do what's right—"

"Kill the cull!" shouted a St Bernard from the front of the crowd. He barked several times to emphasise his point, which caused many people to laugh.

A little girl wearing a bright pink hat tugged on her mother's dress. "It's like the dog heard the lady," she said.

"Indeed," responded the mother, internally amused by the seemingly ridiculous notion. *A dog that speaks human language? As if!*

Ellie continued talking, "We are here to do what's right for badgers – and ourselves. You see," Ellie continued, her voice now booming, "this planet belongs to ALL of us: human and animal alike. To share it, we must consider the needs of other individuals. And other species. We humans often believe that we're guardians of the world, but guardians don't allow the needless slaughter of their fellow inhabitants."

Boo couldn't help but glance over her shoulder to catch a glimpse of Eloise. The kind badger had tears streaming down her face. It took every ounce of willpower to resist leaping down to console her friend, but Boo knew that she needed to continue prompting Ellie.

Boo slowed down the pace as she breathed the next sentence into Ellie's ear, for it was one of the most important lines in the speech.

"Saving badgers means stopping the cull, and stopping the cull means saving ourselves."

"Amen!" yelled a pigeon flitting through the sky. "Preach, sister!"

"This campaign is a mere starting point," said Ellie while pacing across the front of the stage. "It's step one of a wider strategy focused on safeguarding the planet for future generations… of badgers." As she said this, Ellie paused, turned around, and pointed at Eloise.

"And cats," continued Ellie as she rubbed her head against Boo.

Then Ellie pointed at herself, adding, "And humans."

"And mice!" squealed a fluffy house mouse.

"Don't forget swans!" yelled Muhammad from beside the Thames.

"We're in this together!" Ellie shouted, sending the crowd into a roar of claps and chants. "All for one, and one for all!"

This was Bruno the blue tit's cue. He fluttered towards the stage, landed on Ellie's head, and opened his wings like a symphony conductor raising his baton into the air.

Bruno's beak opened, and out poured an elegant melody. His pitch was perfect.

People and animals of all shapes and colours began singing the lyrics Bruno published online:

> *They're black and white*
> *And out of sight,*
> *But Britain's badgers deserve what's right.*

With the event live-streamed on social media, audiences around the world were able to experience the powerful, multi-species collaboration taking place in London.

People in Botswana, Texas, and Venezuela hummed along to the tune while considering the plight of wildlife in their corners of the world.

Meanwhile, inside the Houses of Parliament, eight undecided MPs who'd gathered for a pre-debate conference stopped discussing the merits of the cull, walked over to a nearby window, and watched as the crowd moved apart and came together in the shape of a giant heart.

Of course, they could only hear lyrics coming from the mouths of people – for them, animal protesters were barking, chirping, meowing, and mooing – but they were in awe of what they saw. Words are one thing; actions are another. And, as we all know, the latter are loudest.

They looked at one another and, without saying a word, came to a unanimous decision: they would vote for legislation banning badger culls.

In a dusty corner, shrouded by shadows, a family of mice squealed with delight. The patriarch, Percy, ran into the family home to send a message to Lord Brown, who'd instructed all of his Parliamentary peers to report back with news.

As soon as Lord Brown received word, he sent a text message to Martha, who was still standing on the stage with Boo, Ellie, and Eloise. *Breaking news: undecided MPs to vote for cull ban. Spread the word.*

Martha was so excited to read her uncle's message, she nearly jumped out of her skin. She rushed towards Ellie and Boo with lightning speed, shouting Boo's name the entire way, but Boo couldn't hear her calls over the sound of Bruno's anthem.

Martha tugged on Ellie's trousers, but Ellie didn't respond, so she decided to hike up Ellie's body as Boo had earlier.

By the time she reached Ellie's waist, human and cat alike had noticed Martha and looked down to face her.

"Is everything okay?" Boo asked.

"It's more than okay," responded Martha. "It's WONDERFUL. The cull is off! The eight undecided MPs are so overwhelmed by the protest, they've announced their intention to vote for legislation banning badger culls."

Ellie looked at Boo and Boo at Ellie, neither of them saying a word.

It was as if time stood still; they couldn't hear music dancing in the air or see protesters encircling the stage. They were only aware of each other. In that moment, Boo and Ellie felt like they were back in the Cambridge animal shelter seeing each other for the very first time.

You did it, thought Ellie. *You halted the cull.*

No, we did it, said Boo, without speaking a word.

Language is a powerful tool, as the protesters well know, but not all communication requires it.

Boo began purring so loudly, the megaphone transmitted her rumbling to the crowd, which had, seconds earlier, fallen quiet after Bruno clapped his wings against his body to signify the song's end.

Boo leaned towards Ellie. "I reckon we'd better share the good news?"

Ellie raised the megaphone to her mouth for the last time and shouted, "We did it! We killed the cull!"

The crowd went wild. Dogs barked, people hugged, and birds zipped through the air in celebratory swirls. A sense of camaraderie flooded the city's cobbled streets, riverside pathways, and historic buildings. Like a cat warming itself on sunlit stones, London basked in its afterglow for days to come.

Ellie put the megaphone down and took Boo from her shoulder, raising her fluffy body into the air like Rafiki thrusting Simba high above the African savannah.

EPILOGUE

It's 5th July 2020, and the Kenyan sun blazes bright as Boo slips out of her and Ellie's tent to look for her new feline friend.

She wades into the savannah's tawny grasses like a swimmer into a lake. Her senses are on high alert as she strides towards the Ewaso Nyiro River. It's empty this time of year – it hasn't felt the soft touch of rain for months – but the members of the Ewaso lion pride remain in its orbit. It's their favourite place in all of Samburu, partly because their ancestors have called it home for centuries. They are kings of the river and queens of the savannah, and until recently, no one could touch them – neither the strongest man nor the wildest beast – but things have begun to change.

Boo first learnt about lion poaching when Ellie wrote her second term essay, the very thing that brought them here. Coupled with her efforts halting the badger cull, it caused Ellie's professors to notice her. Of course, they didn't know that Ellie's success stemmed from Boo's ingenuity and her network of animal activists, but they recognised Ellie's passion and decided that she was the ideal candidate for a six-month internship researching lion populations in Kenya.

When Ellie told Boo about the opportunity, Boo felt anxious and upset. She was finally feeling settled in Cambridge and didn't want to abandon her new friends or their conservation work, which rapidly expanded after Parliament officially banned badger culls in early March. However, Boo quickly learnt that life in Kenya would involve a type of wilderness the young cat had never known.

There aren't just birds, small mammals, and insects – there are big and powerful creatures: lions, elephants, giraffes, and rhinos. And Boo and Ellie don't live in an enclosed flat. In the Samburu National Reserve, they sleep in a large tent whose canvas flaps led to a wild world full of storybook magic.

It is dangerous, too, which Ellie CONSTANTLY mentions to Boo. If Ellie had her way, the tabby would never venture far from their tent or the research station where Ellie works each day.

But, as we all know, Ellie doesn't always get her way.

Boo has an important message to deliver to the Ewaso pride's alpha male, and, with Ellie out on anti-poaching patrols, she has just enough time to reach him and return home without Ellie's knowledge.

Boo reaches the edge of the river. She turns her body, looks in every direction, and glances up and into the sky. No birds of prey this morning.

Boo meows with as much might as she can muster before tiptoeing down the river's sandy banks.

Suddenly, movement – the flick of a tail or twitch of a whisker – followed by a roar.

A guttural call for friend or foe.

Boo smiles, confident in the knowledge that she's the former, and walks towards its source.